THE
REPUBLIC
of
BIRDS

Amulet Books
New York

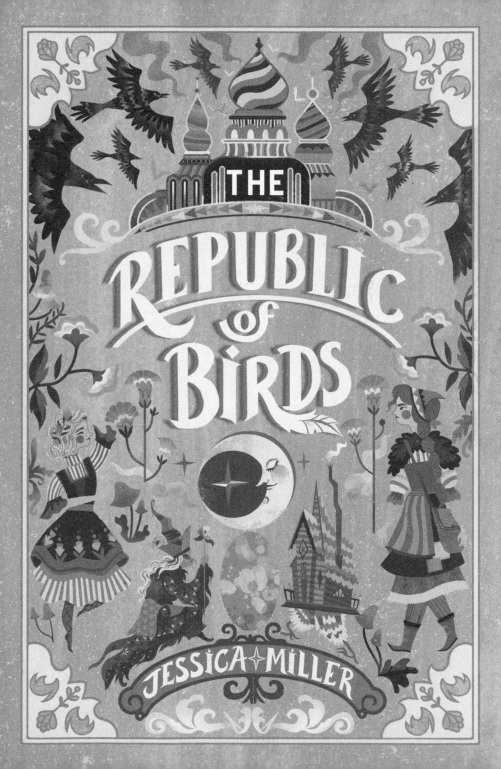

THE
REPUBLIC
OF
BIRDS

JESSICA MILLER

Cataloging-in-Publication Data has been applied for and may be obtained from the Library of Congress.

ISBN 978-1-4197-3675-9

Text copyright © 2021 Jessica Miller
Jacket illustrations copyright © 2021 Karl James Mountford
Book design by Marcie Lawrence

Printed and bound in U.S.A.
10 9 8 7 6 5 4 3 2 1

Amulet Books are available at special discounts when purchased in quantity for premiums and promotions as well as fundraising or educational use. Special editions can also be created to specification. For details, contact specialsales@abramsbooks.com or the address below.

ABRAMS The Art of Books
195 Broadway, New York, NY 10007
abramsbooks.com

FOR MY SISTERS, ZOË AND CHARLOTTE

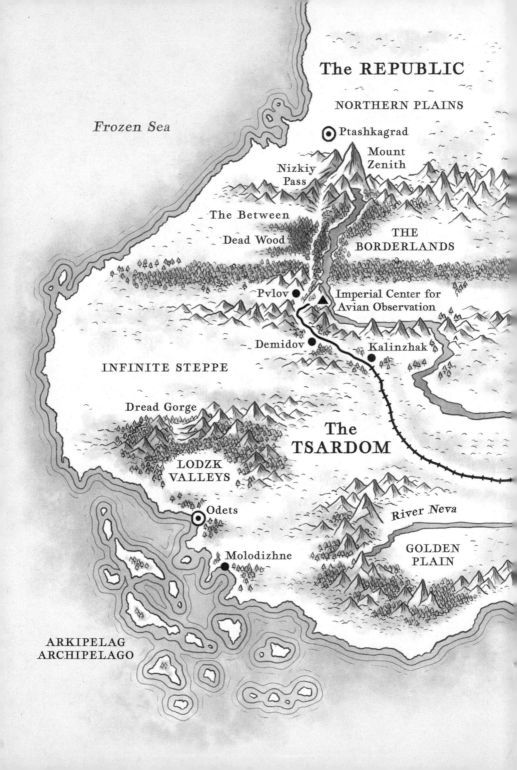

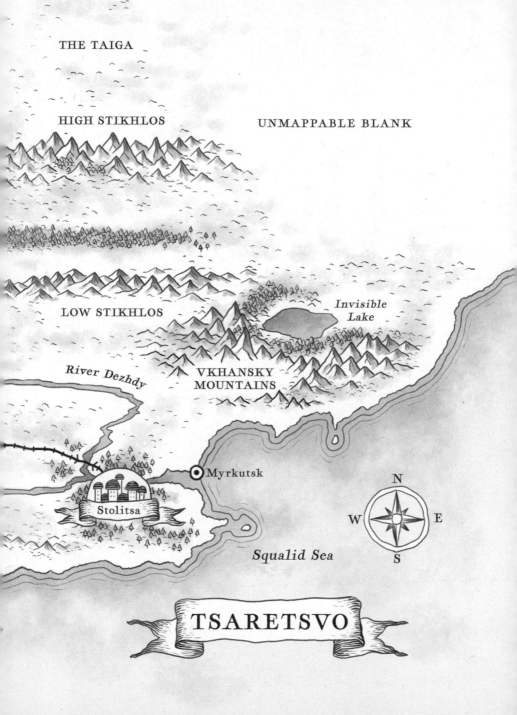

Before the War in the Skies, before the map of Tsaretsvo was sliced in two and divided into the human Tsardom and the Republic of Birds, birds and humans lived in peace. In Stolitsa, the Cloud Palace floated over the Stone Palace with cumulus turrets and battlements of nimbus. In the Cloud Palace lived the Avian Counsel. In the Stone Palace lived the tsars and tsarinas. The palaces ruled Tsaretsvo together, and birds and humans lived alongside each other. Birds large and small nested in the trees in the Mikhailovsky Garden and splashed in its fountains in summer. Songbirds sang with the orchestra at the Mariinsky Theatre. Peacocks adorned the city walls.

Birds and humans shared the earth and the sky. And if it hadn't been for the Great Mapping, things might have continued in this way. But in 1817, Tsarina Pyotrovna decreed that every corner in the land must be mapped to show the broad expanse of her Tsardom.

The Great Cartographers journeyed forth, and, with the exception of the Unmappable Blank, they charted every corner of the land. Krylnikov mapped the Arkhipelag Archipelago. Belugov traced the shores of the Frozen Sea. Karelin found the source of the River Dezhdy high in the Stikhlo Mountains.

In 1822, Golovnin set out for the Infinite Steppe, where it was rumored firebirds still nested amid the tussocks and streaked through the skies. And in 1824, he returned to the Stone Palace, carrying a firebird's egg in his pocket . . .

—*Glorious Victory: An Impartial Account of the War in the Skies* by I. P. Pavlova, chapter one: "The Firebird's Egg."

INTO EXILE

The train starts down the tracks. Through the window, the station slides away. We are leaving Stolitsa—our home—behind us.

We might not be back for a long time.

We might not be back at all.

Father sits beside me. He holds the memo from the Stone Palace in his hand. I crane my neck to read it:

Attn: Aleksei Oblomov

In recognition of your exemplary service as head architect for the Sky Metro, Tsarina Yekaterina has appointed you Minister for Avian Intelligence, effective immediately. Her Imperial Highness has afforded you and your family the honor of a military escort to the Imperial Center for Avian Observation. You are to depart at your earliest convenience. I congratulate you on this promotion on behalf of the tsarina.

—Ivan Dementievsky, Imperial Undersecretary

"This promotion," says the memo. But even I know Father isn't being promoted. It was all over yesterday's papers. "Grand Opening for the Sky Metro Delayed!" reported the *Stolitsa Zhournal*. "Head Architect Oblomov accepts responsibility for mismeasurements. Tsarina Yekaterina has expressed her disappointment."

And now, Father is being sent—politely, painlessly—into exile. And we are being exiled with him.

The snowy outline of the city slips past. I see the domed roofs of the Stone Palace, the bare winter trees in the Mikhailovsky Garden, the gates of the Instructionary Institute for Girls. I wonder whether I'll ever walk through those gates again.

Above the roofline, I see the military balloons and zeppelins, some drifting and some moored. I see the Floating Birch Forest Tea Room and the rails of the Sky Metro, still unfinished.

The train rushes onward, and the city grows smaller. For a while, I can still make out the sign for the Floating Birch Forest Tea Room, a neon-pink samovar blinking high up in the air, but the clouds thicken and then even that is gone.

Father clears his throat and smooths his moustache. A speech is coming. I have spent nearly thirteen years trying to avoid Father's speeches. I know the signs.

"Our lives," he announces, "will be very different now."

At this statement, Anastasia bursts into jangling tears. She has been bursting into tears at regular intervals ever since the two soldiers who make up our military escort appeared in the front parlor this morning. And she is jangling because she spent fourteen of the fifteen minutes we were given to gather our belongings piling every piece of jewelry she owns onto her person. Her fingers are stacked with rings, and her neck has disappeared under strings of diamonds and pearls that clink and clank together as she cries.

Father pats her hand, and Mira rushes across the carriage to throw her slender arms around Anastasia.

"Don't cry," says Mira. "At least we'll all be together."

Mira is always nice to Anastasia. Mira is always nice to everyone. Everyone loves Mira.

She strokes Anastasia's arm and says, "Don't cry, Mother."

Calling her "Mother" is taking nice too far, if you ask me. Anastasia is our stepmother.

After a while, Anastasia stops sobbing and starts whimpering picturesquely instead. She wobbles her lip and flutters her lashes and makes her eyes into two wells of deep, brave sorrow, just as she did in the final scene of *Bride of the Wolves*, when her husband, the noble Wolf King, is shot by hunters. Picturesque whimpering, according to Stolitsa's cinema critics, is Anastasia's greatest dramatic talent.

Father smooths his moustache some more and goes on with his speech.

"Our lives," he repeats, "are going to be very different."

"Drastically different," says Anastasia. "No shops. No theaters. No zeppelin rides. Hardly any fresh caviar, either, I shouldn't expect."

"No ballet lessons," adds Mira in a sad voice. Mira loves dancing exactly as much as I hate dancing, which is to say that Mira loves dancing with her whole heart.

"No ballet lessons," says Father. "No caviar. And besides all that . . . well, there are certain creatures—unsavory creatures—who have been unwelcome in Tsaretsvo ever since the War in the Skies." He smooths his moustache again. If he smooths it any more, he's going to smooth it right off his face. "We might expect to see . . . creatures that we're not accustomed to seeing in the city."

"Creatures?" I ask. "Do you mean yagas?"

"Yes, Olga," he sighs. "We might expect to see"—his lip curls as if the word has an evil taste—"yagas."

I have read all about yagas in my school history book, *Glorious*

Victory: An Impartial Account of the War in the Skies. Yagas are magi-cal, but more than this they are cunning and dangerous. It was their wicked deceit that started the War in the Skies. For centuries, the tsars and tsarinas relied on the magical advice of their Imperial Coven, a group of the most powerful yagas in the land. But Tsarina Pyotrovna's Coven was tempted by the firebird's egg. They stole it for themselves, then vanished. And as punishment for the Coven's trickery, every yaga in Tsaretsvo was driven out. There have been no yagas, and no magic, in Tsaretsvo since. But it is rumored that yagas can still be found at the fringes of the Tsardom, in the Borderlands. From what Father is saying, it seems the rumors are true.

"Yagas!" wails Anastasia. "This is the last straw, Aleksei! Are we to live surrounded by those nasty, unnatural hags? It makes me ill to think of them in their dirty, chicken-legged huts, with their long yellow fingernails and their—"

"Hush," snaps Father, and he jerks his head toward Mira, who has pulled her curly hair loose from her plait. She twists a strand of it around her little finger. Mira twists her hair like this when she is anxious.

I reach over and untwist it, and when Mira leans into me, I shift along the seat to make room for her. With a wobble in her voice, she says, "I've heard yagas eat the meat off children's bones. I've heard they use the bones for toothpicks when they're done."

"You mustn't believe everything you hear," says Father gently. "But yes. Yagas can be dangerous. We will need to be careful."

I am not as anxious as Mira. I know yagas are dangerous and mean and sly and that they have long yellow fingernails, just like Anastasia says, but all the same, it would be a terrific thrill to see one.

Father smooths his moustache for a long time. When he has finished, he says, "And of course, there are the birds."

The birds.

I have never seen a bird. But one afternoon years ago in the library of the Instructionary Institute for Girls, I opened an old book of Tsarish history. The birds had been carefully removed from all the books from before the War in the Skies. Sentences were blacked out, sometimes whole paragraphs. Engraved illustrations had been cut, leaving holes that, I guessed, were bird-shaped in patches of sky and branches of trees.

But in this book, I came across a picture the librarian's scissors had missed.

A flock of birds against a cloud in the night sky.

I leaned in to see their stretched wings, their seed eyes, their delicately tensed claws. I wondered what their feathers felt like to touch and what sounds they made as they flew through the sky.

I hunched over the book and coughed loudly to cover the sound as I tore out the page. I folded it and tucked it into my pocket. Later, when I was alone, I took it out and looked at the picture and wondered if the sky had ever been so busy with birds. I wondered if they could really be as large as they appeared in the picture, their wings spread so wide they stretched across the moon.

Anastasia caught me, and she burned the picture in the parlor fire.

I rest my head against the train window. I close my eyes and try to remember the birds in the picture: their long, sharp beaks, the way they filled the sky.

A rap at our carriage door jolts me awake. The train is stopped at—I squint through the window to read the station sign—Kalinzhak.

Kalinzhak, one-half of our military escort informs us, is the end of the line.

"Have we arrived, then?" asks Anastasia as she is helped down from the carriage.

Her question is answered by the unceremonious dumping of our trunks onto the platform. The train moves off, back in the direction from which it came, trailing gusts of soot that settle blackly on the snowdrifts banked on either side of the tracks.

Father takes a letter from his pocket. "Train travel past Kalinzhak is not possible before the snow melts," he reads. "We go by sled to Demidov, where we will be met by the departing Minister for Avian Intelligence—a man by the name of Krupnik—who will take us the rest of the way."

"A sled," mutters Anastasia into the collar of her white mink coat. "How primitive."

The sled is long and narrow. It is drawn by twelve dogs so white they would disappear into the snow if they weren't marked out by their black eyes and noses. It is the kind of sled that promises adventure—the same kind of sled that Belugov traveled on when he mapped the edges of the Frozen Sea. I am about to tell Mira this, when I remember that, while the sled and the dogs made it back to Stolitsa, Belugov did not.

Passengers mill around, waiting for the driver to harness the dogs. Anastasia is busy brushing snowflakes from the shoulders of her snow-white mink. She enlists Father to help her. I count our trunks as they're loaded onto the back of the sled. And Mira—

Where is Mira?

I whip my head around.

Mira is lying in the snow.

"Look!" she says, leaping up. "It's almost perfect." She points to where she was lying, at a snow angel.

"You make one," she says. "Yours are always better than mine."

I am almost thirteen years old. Too old for snow angels, really. But the snow is so white and so clean and so fresh. When a flake lands on my tongue, it tastes of pine, unlike the snow in Stolitsa, which turns gritty and gray almost as soon as it has fallen. "There's no time," I say as Mira runs toward me and pushes me so I fall back onto the cold, powdery snow. I flap my arms and legs, and the shape of an angel appears around me. Mira hauls me up, and we admire the impressions we have left in the snow.

We make more snow angels, laughing like we did when we were little, until the crack of a whip in the air jolts me upright. We shake the snow from our clothes and sprint back to the sled and into the only seats left, one on either side of an old lady with a face as wrinkled as a walnut shell and a ring of silver keys on a chain around her neck. From her pocket, she takes half a raw onion and a paper twist of salt. She lets the salt fall onto the onion just like the snow that is starting to fall from the sky.

With a crunch of onion and a second crack of the driver's whip, we start. The dogs pelt through the snow, and the forest slaps the sled as we fly along. The first time a branch comes at me, I end up with a snow-dripping mouthful of pine needles. I'm still spitting the needles out when I see the second branch. This time, I duck.

For a moment, the sled is airborne, and then we land with a long skid on a frozen river. The River Dezhdy. I have always loved the chapter in *Great Names in Tsarish Cartography* where Karelin travels up the Dezhdy to discover its source high in the Stikhlo Mountains, catching trout with his dagger to sustain himself as his weeks on the river stretch into months.

The dogs patter over the river's glassy surface. I am beginning to enjoy the ride, when I feel prodding between my shoulder blades. I turn around, and Anastasia thrusts a cold handful of diamonds and silver at me.

"Put these in your pockets," she hisses. "Where no one can see them."

"Why?" I hiss back.

"People"—she closes her coat over her necklaces—"are looking. We'll be robbed if we're not careful."

I snort. People are looking because Anastasia, tinseled with jewels, looks like a Christmas tree.

"Did you just snort at me?"

"No!" I lie. "And besides, they're probably only looking at you because they recognize you from one of your movies."

"You may be right," she says. "*The Glass Wife* was very popular with Northern audiences."

She relaxes. I think she even begins to enjoy the furtive glances of other passengers.

"Strezhevoy!" yells the driver as the sled glides to a halt. A beet-faced man in a sheepskin coat clambers over the other passengers and lands next to the sled in a puff of snow.

After we pull away from Strezhevoy, I hear snapping sounds from deep in the belly of the forest. They are soft to begin with, but they quickly grow louder. Soon, it sounds like the splintering of boughs torn from trees. One or two of the other passengers glance toward the forest, but no one behaves as if these strange noises are anything out of the ordinary, least of all the woman sitting between Mira and me. She stares ahead and chews her onion in a slow, contemplative kind of way. But the noises make my stomach churn. When I imagine the beast that could possibly make such a sound, I imagine something large. Something with fur and claws and teeth.

Mira reaches her hand around the back of the onion woman. Her gloved fingers find mine.

The noises are getting louder and closer.

Behind me, Anastasia smothers a gasp as a wooden hut perched on a pair of pink scaly chicken feet lurches out of the trees. The tiles on its roof are so loose that they ripple in the wind, and its walls are stippled with dark green–black moss. It's not as fearsome looking as the pictures I have seen in my history books; it doesn't have a fence made of bones, for one thing, or a fire–breathing horse tied to its gatepost. Apart from its chicken feet, it looks almost ordinary, in a dilapidated sort of way. But still. There's no mistaking what it is—or what's sure to be inside.

The hut comes closer, and I feel myself prickling all over—with fear, certainly, but also with a spiky excitement. Am I about to see a real, live yaga?

The other passengers are calm, almost bored looking, as if they see yagas every other day of the week. But Anastasia has covered her eyes with her diamond–encrusted fingers, and her shoulders are shaking. Mira's eyes brim with frightened tears. Even Father looks afraid. His moustache trembles at its corners.

What is *wrong* with me? I shouldn't be excited. I definitely shouldn't *look* excited. Girls have been sent to Bleak Steppe for less. I wobble my lip and wring my hands. I'm not as good an actress as Anastasia, but I think it will do.

"Is it . . . ?" asks Mira.

"It is," I say.

"No need to panic," says Father in a low voice. "Eyes ahead, Olga."

I turn my face forward, but from the corner of my eye, I can see almost everything.

The hut's window is hidden behind rotting wooden shutters, but all at once, the shutters fall open. As if by magic, I think. And then I think, well, of course by magic. It is a yaga's hut, after all.

A face pokes out from behind yellowed lace curtains. The yaga is nothing like the illustrations I have seen in books. She doesn't have eyes the color of blood or iron teeth. She looks almost ordinary.

"Tell your fortune in a match!" she cries. "Two kopecks! Find your fate in the flame!"

The sled stops, and some of the passengers climb out, fumbling in their pockets for coins.

"Look directly ahead," says Father in a tight voice. "This unfortunate display will soon be over."

But this time, I turn to watch. How many chances will I have in my life to see a yaga's magic?

The yaga pulls a match out of her box. She doesn't strike it. She whispers to it instead in a voice that sounds like the rasping of tinder. And the match lights. Its flame is purple tinged, and it dances from side to side. The yaga bends down and whispers into her customer's ear.

I want to know what she sees in the fire. I wonder what she is whispering. But she is too far away for me to hear. I feel obscurely disappointed. The first time I see a yaga, and I hardly *see* her at all.

The passengers bundle back into the sled. The whip cracks, and we start to move again.

Soon the hut will be gone. It will be a relief, I tell myself, when the hut is gone. A relief and nothing more.

But the hut scrambles along the ice, trying to keep up with the sled dogs. "Tell your fortune in a match!" cries the yaga. "Read your fate in a flame!"

The hut draws level with the sled. The yaga leans out the window. Her face is very close to mine. My excitement has seeped away, and only fear remains. Why has she chosen *me* to address? Can she tell what I was thinking? Can she sense that I was curious?

"Tell your fortune in a match," she coaxes. I smell her breath and recoil, but she just leans even closer. "Don't you want to find out what the future holds?" she asks.

"Don't answer, Olga," warns Father. "Pretend you can't hear it."

I say nothing.

"You do want to know, don't you? Tell you what," she says. "I'll do you for free."

I can feel my heartbeat, thick and heavy, pounding through my blood. The yaga is wrong. I don't want to know, not at all.

She slides a match from the box. The flame leaps upright even though we are moving at quite a speed. But the woman with the onion grabs her by the wrist and pulls the yaga's face close to her own. She whispers something too soft for me to hear, and the yaga spits on the match, and it fizzles. Then she draws her head inside the hut. The shutters snap shut, and the hut slinks back into the trees.

"Tawdry tricks," mutters the old woman before returning her attention to her onion.

Mira leans across the woman. "Are you all right, Olga?" she asks. "Weren't you scared?"

Was I scared? How can I answer? I felt something so much more complicated than simple fear. I wait for my heart to slow to its regular speed before I say, "Yes. I was scared. But she's gone now."

"She's gone," sniffs Anastasia, "but she came awfully close to you. You'll need to wash as soon as we arrive at the Center."

"I don't think it's contagious," I say.

"You can't be too careful, Olga," says Father.

The driver calls out the stops as we pass them: "Grizhelov!" and "Kibirsk!" and "Roslow!"

Some of the places are small villages. Others are just signposts in the snow near paths that disappear into the forest. By the time we reach Demidov, which appears to be nothing but a signpost and a tumbledown wooden shelter, only the woman with the onion is left with us in the sled. She collects her paper-wrapped parcels, nods goodbye, and disappears. Her keys jingle as she goes.

We alight into the snow with our trunks, and the driver cracks his whip one final time, and the dogs draw the sled back down the river, out of sight.

Sunk beneath snowdrifts is an empty wooden shelter. We go inside to wait for Krupnik. It feels like we are the only people left in the world.

CHAPTER TWO

THE GREAT CARTOGRAPHERS

Snow swirls outside the wooden shelter. We sit inside in the cold. The cracks in the walls have been stuffed with sheepskin and straw to keep the wind out, but they are no match for its knifing gusts. Even in the cramped space, Mira begins to dance. Father and Anastasia watch her adoringly. I ignore her and take *Great Names in Tsarish Cartography* from my coat pocket.

I have loved the stories of the Great Cartographers ever since I can remember, though I loved them more before I realized that cartography is not meant for girls, that all the cartographers in the Imperial Society for Cartography are men. When I was young, I read these stories and dreamed of being a cartographer, that one day I might cross the Vkhansky Mountains or circumnavigate the Invisible Lake or even map the Unmappable Blank.

Now, I think of them as wonderful stories that happen to other people. Still, I sometimes take the long way to the Instructionary Institute for Girls just so I can stop at the gates of the Imperial Society for Cartography and wonder about what goes on behind them.

Here in the wooden shelter in the snow, I start to read about Krylnikov charting the Arkhipelag Archipelago off the south Tsarish coast, but it feels wrong to read about the sunbaked islands in this bone-twinging cold. I flip to chapter fourteen, in which Golovnin travels to the Infinite Steppe, but thinking about Golovnin makes me think about the firebird's egg, which makes me think about the War in the Skies, and here at the edge of the Tsardom, the War feels much more real than it did in my history lessons at the Instructionary Institute. I quickly go back to my favorite chapter, chapter seventeen: "A Tragic Failure: Londonov's Attempt to Map the Unmappable Blank." I don't need to read the book. I know this chapter by heart:

In the Great Mapping, every region of Tsaretsvo was charted and added to the official map of the Tsardom. Except for one: the Unmappable Blank, an icy region thought to lie to the north of the Northern Plains. None of the cartographers who had entered the Unmappable Blank had ever returned. There were rumors—wholly unscientific rumors—that it was an enchanted place where compasses spun wildly and sextants couldn't find the horizon. And yet, Boris Londonov's announcement in the spring of 1829 that he would mount an expedition to the Blank was greeted with optimism. After all, Londonov was the greatest cartographer of the age. It was Londonov who had pinpointed the coordinates of the Invisible Lake, and Londonov who had scaled Mount Zenith, the highest peak in the High Stikhlos. It was even said that when Karelin finally completed his journey up the Dezhdy, he found one of Londonov's monogrammed handkerchiefs at the river's source. If anyone could map the Unmappable Blank, it was Londonov . . .

"Ouch!" I cry, almost dropping the book.

Mira's left boot has connected with the side of my head. "Is this really the best place to practice your pirouette?" I ask.

"It's an arabesque," says Mira. "Not a pirouette. *This* is a pirouette." She tucks one leg up, clasps her hands in front of her, and spins.

I bite down a sigh. I don't like watching Mira dance. Not because Mira is a bad dancer; she dances like the air is water and she is floating in it. And not because I'm jealous, either, even though I could be very jealous that Mira is graceful and charming and almost certain to become a prima ballerina at the Mariinsky Theatre as soon as she's old enough, while I am graceless and charmless and entirely not balletic.

Maybe I am a little jealous. I know I'll never be good at anything in the way that Mira is good at dancing, and knowing that makes me sad.

I frown down at my book, only half watching as Mira spins. She finishes the pirouette by flinging her arms out with a flourish and unleashing a shower of dirty straw from the ceiling.

I glare at her and spit straw from my mouth.

"Sorry," she says in a very unsorry voice. "Madame Tansevat says I must practice every day." Mira smiles at me, and her smug expression makes me want to kick her sharply in the shins.

I don't kick her, of course. I just say, "I hardly think Madame Tansevat would want you to practice here."

I look to Father for support, but he shows no sign that he has heard. He is unfolding the telegram from the palace. As soon as he is finished, he refolds it. Unfolds it. Refolds it. Something about him seems smaller.

Beside him, Anastasia counts on her fingers. "The porcelain dogs," she murmurs. "The amber binoculars." She is listing the contents of our Stolitsa apartment. Everything we couldn't take with us. "The harmonium. Yerzhei, the butler."

"Sergei, the butler," I correct her. Yerzhei was two butlers before Sergei.

"At least I have my mink," she says, and wraps herself tighter in the snowy-white folds of her prized fur. But even the mink proves small comfort, and she continues with some gloomy predictions. "They'll recast *The Ghost in the Lantern* if I'm not back for rehearsals," she says, and then she narrows her eyes. "Valentina Chershkova will pounce on my part, mark my words. And Olga!" She clutches Father's arm. "Oh, Aleksei! What if . . . what if Olga misses her Spring Blossom Ball?"

The Spring Blossom Ball is the social event of the season. Each spring, in the year of their thirteenth birthdays, the daughters of Stolitsa's best families are presented at court. And this year is my year. Our last rehearsal was this past Tuesday. It did not go well. Not for me.

After the Grand Procession, in which the Spring Blossoms make their entrance, and before the dancing—the less said about the dancing, the better—comes the talent. On the night of the ball, each Blossom performs a talent for the audience. A talent that shows her to her best advantage. It helps, of course, if she has an advantage to show. At the start of that Tuesday rehearsal, my talent was fan waving. Monsieur Palanquin had decided on fan waving for me because I was too inelegant for ribbon twirling, too artless for flower arranging, and too tuneless to play the Tsarish national anthem on a set of small silver bells. But, as Monsieur Palanquin observed at the Tuesday rehearsal, even standing still and waving a fan was too much for me. After muttering that he had never seen such a feeble flutter, he assigned me epic poetry, which, as everyone knows, is a last-resort kind of talent. I spent the rest of the rehearsal memorizing "The Clouds Were Stained with Blood: An Ode to the Memory of the War in the Skies."

So when Anastasia begins to wail about the possibility of my missing the Spring Blossom Ball, I don't manage to look as remorseful as she expects me to.

"Do you know what I think, Olga?" she snaps. "I think you're glad to miss the Spring Blossom Ball. We've been struck by misfortune—sent to the end of the Earth—and you're glad!"

Mira chooses this moment to do another arabesque and loosen another wad of straw from the ceiling.

"Do you really think I'm glad to be here?" I ask Anastasia. "In the middle of nowhere, with a scalp full of cold straw?"

"I don't know," she shoots back. "Are you?"

I press my lips together and stare hard through a crack in the wall. Snow is falling so hard outside that it's impossible to tell where the white sky stops and the white ground begins. I know I wasn't glad to be in Stolitsa, where I was expected to dress prettily and behave prettily and spend hours fluttering a fan while the students at the Instructionary Institute for Boys got to learn Latin and geometry and cartography. Especially cartography. I *was* at least a little glad to leave the city, where I had never felt like I belonged.

Here it's all so different. Different and exciting and terrifying and confusing. Here there are sleds drawn by white fluffy dogs, and there are yagas—real, live yagas. And, I suppose, somewhere in the sky, there are birds.

Am I glad to be here? I really can't say. I guess I'm in what *Great Names in Tsarish Cartography* would describe as uncharted territory.

CHAPTER THREE

THE IMPERIAL CENTER FOR AVIAN OBSERVATION

Mira is first to see Krupnik. She is peering through one of the cracks in the wall. I press my eye up next to hers and look out. We watch as the blurry speck in the snow slowly takes the shape of a man astride a—

"Did you ever see such an odd horse?" exclaims Mira. "So small. And with such stubby legs!"

"It's a tarpan," I tell her. "You only find them in the North. Belugov mapped the Northern Plains from the back of a tarpan."

Krupnik leads other tarpans on a rope behind him. We count as—one, two, three, four—they emerge from the blizzard.

When Krupnik reaches the hut, he dismounts and cries, "Oblomov!" He steps inside and presses Father's hand. He wears a ragged bearskin coat and a wide grin, and he has a gingery beard that reaches his knees.

"Well," says Krupnik, and he claps his hands. "I'm sure you're anxious to get to your new home."

No one answers him. Undeterred, he trudges outside, lifts our trunks onto the back of one of the tarpans, and ties them fast.

"Aleksei"—Anastasia's nails dig into Father's sleeve—"you don't think he means for us to ride those . . . those . . ."

I smile into my coat collar. Anastasia's biography, *From Steppe to Star: The Anastasia Krasnoyarska Story*, makes much of the fact that Anastasia was abandoned on the Steppe as a baby and raised by a herd of wild tarpans until the age of fourteen. It's all nonsense, of course; Studio Kino-Otleechno devises ridiculous romantic backstories for all its stars. Anastasia was no more raised by wild tarpans than Valentina Chershkova sneezes pearls. Not that Anastasia would ever admit it.

I arrange my face in a puzzled expression, and, all innocence, I say, "I thought you would have a special affinity for tarpans. You were raised by a herd of them, after all."

"Naturally, I do," says Anastasia, and in an instant, her manner changes to somewhere between haughtiness and calm. She climbs astride the closest tarpan, looking almost as if she knows what she is doing. She and the tarpan toss their manes in unison. I have to hand it to her: She is an excellent actress.

We start off into the foothills of the mountains.

I jolt along in my saddle as the tarpan trots over the rocky terrain. We jolt like this for a very long time. So long my eyes start to stream from the cold and my lashes turn stiff and frosty.

A ramshackle town clinging to the side of the slope finally comes into view, and Anastasia lifts her head. "Are we here?" she asks.

Krupnik answers with a laugh. "That's Pvlov," he says. "It's a garrison town—the northernmost town in the whole Tsardom. Tsarina Yekaterina's XVIII Imperial Regiment is stationed there. But it's not the Center for Avian Observation." He points up to the place where the slope turns treeless and icy. "*There's* the Center."

He slaps the reins of his tarpan, and it snorts. Its warm breath mists in the air.

We pass Pvlov. The forest thins, and the mountain grows bald. At the very top of the slope is a curious construction: a wooden house high on stilts. Low clouds swirl around it. "There," says Krupnik. "The Imperial Center for Avian Observation."

Below it on the slope is an old manor house. It looks like it might have been grand once. Now it is weathered and crumbling. A meager vegetable garden wilts under the snow. At the back of the garden, a thin white goat nibbles what stubble it can find between the rocks and ice. A lace curtain in a window twitches as we ride past.

"Your arrival hasn't gone unmarked," says Krupnik.

"I thought there was nothing here but the Center," says Father.

"You're not quite alone," says Krupnik, and he jerks his thumb at the manor house. "Those are your neighbors at Tsarina Yekaterina's Beneficent Home for Retired Ladies-in-Waiting. You'll meet them before long, I shouldn't wonder."

The Center is so high on the steep ridge that it can be reached only by a ladder, which wobbles as I climb it. When we arrive, cloud-damp and wind-rumpled, at the top, Krupnik ushers us into a shabby entrance hall. He introduces us to his wife, Larisa Dmitrovna, and then to Colonel Pritnip, head of the Pvlov garrison. Larisa Dmitrovna is a faded-looking woman wearing an afternoon dress. It is trimmed in rich velvet but made in a style that passed from fashion several seasons ago. Anastasia looks at Larisa Dmitrovna's dress with alarm, taking in its voluminous sleeves and its old-fashioned flouncing. I know she is making the same calculations as I am. Just how long have the Krupniks been here?

Krupnik proposes that he and Pritnip take Father on a tour of the Center. Larisa looks reluctant to leave the entrance hall, where all her trunks are stacked and from which she can see the tarpans waiting below to carry her to Demidov. Eventually, she invites us to take tea in a cramped room that she describes optimistically as the parlor.

Anastasia, equally optimistic, looks for a maid to bring out the tea trolley, but Larisa fetches the samovar and pours the tea herself. Then she settles on a three-legged chair and says with a watery smile, "And these must be your daughters."

"Stepdaughters," I tell her through a mouthful of dusty biscuit. I ignore Anastasia's glare.

"This is Olga," says Anastasia. "She is preparing for her Spring Blossom Ball."

"Oh." Larisa looks at me dubiously. Perhaps because, with my top lip speckled with biscuit crumbs, I don't look like Spring Blossom material. I'm wiping the crumbs away from my mouth when I realize that Larisa isn't concerned about whether I'll make a good Spring Blossom. She doubts I'll return to Stolitsa in time for the Spring Blossom Ball at all.

"And this," says Anastasia, "is Mira. Mira is an accomplished ballerina. Only ten, and there's talk of her joining the junior corps at the Mariinsky Theatre."

"How wonderful to have such a talented daughter— stepdaughter," smiles Larisa, and I feel my cheeks glow red. I stare into my teacup.

"We're both talented," says Mira stoutly, "in our own ways."

This is meant to be nice, I know, but it stings. We are not both talented, no matter what Mira says.

"I am so very fond of the ballet," simpers Larisa over the rim of her teacup. "Perhaps, if Mira wouldn't mind . . ."

Mira never minds. And before Larisa has even finished her sentence, she has sprung up from her chair and cleared a space in the parlor.

But I've seen enough of her dancing for today. No one will notice if I slip away.

I poke through the cobwebbed kitchen, and in a corridor leading away from it, I find another ladder. As I stand there, Pritnip's shiny black boot appears on the top rung. I slip back into a shadowy corner of the kitchen and listen.

I hear Pritnip climb down, then Krupnik, and then Father.

"That was the observation deck," says Krupnik. "Impressive, don't you agree?"

"Indeed," says Father.

"Now," continues Krupnik, "if you'll follow me, I'll show you our communications room. It's equipped with the latest in telegram technology and a direct line to the Stone Palace."

The footsteps fade. I creep back out into the corridor and climb the ladder.

The observation deck is a small room. Its walls are made of thick glass, but all I can see through them is a gray soup of cloud. There is a jumble of meteorological equipment—a barometer, an anemometer—in one corner and a large globe in another. Fixed to the center of the ceiling is a periscope. I hold the viewer to my face and angle the periscope away from the cloud, twisting the knob at its side to focus. And, peering through the lens, I see the lines and markings I know so well from the Tsarish map springing to life across the landscape. The mountain we are perched atop is part of a range of mountains. On the Tsarish map, the peaks are stitched together into the blue line that marks the Low Stikhlos and the edge of the Tsardom. I turn the periscope toward the place where the mountains give way to thick forest. This is the Borderlands. Somewhere past the Borderlands, hidden by clouds, are the High Stikhlos, the highest mountains in all Tsaretsvo. Beyond them is the Republic of Birds.

I swivel the periscope westward and look along the line of mountains until they disappear into the distance. Here is the

Infinite Steppe, where Georgei Golovnin found the firebird's egg. I look to the east, where the Unmappable Blank begins. It looks frosty and white and featureless, as blank as the blank space that marks it on the map. I increase the periscope's magnification, but even then there's no way of seeing where the Blank ends or if it ends at all.

It's a strange thrill, seeing the lands from the maps I have pored over so many times. It makes my fingers itch for a pencil and some drafting paper. Perhaps somewhere out there is a bend in the River Dezhdy that no one has noticed before, or an uncharted outcropping of slopes somewhere in the Stikhlos. Something I could add to the map. Something that could secure me a footnote in the history of Tsarish cartography.

I imagine myself sharing a page with Golovnin or Londonov, but almost instantly I blush at my own foolishness. I replace the lens cap on the periscope. I've only been out of Stolitsa a few hours, and I've already forgotten its rules: There are no women in *Great Names in Tsarish Cartography*.

Mira is still dancing when I climb back down the ladder, only now Father and Krupnik and Colonel Pritnip are watching her, too. She dances so beautifully. The glow of the lamp looks like the shine of a spotlight, and the parlor seems to stretch out into a stage.

Mira leaps and twirls. Everyone is so busy watching her that no one notices me, and no one notices the swish of movement outside the window. No one except me sees that a large white creature with a sharp black beak is standing on the windowsill.

The creature—the *bird*—fans its wings. I know I should say something, but I can't stop staring. It is the first time I have seen a real bird. The birds in the library book, the birds in my dreams, were flat and small and dull compared to the creature before me now. This bird has bright red legs, and the feathers of her white wings turn black at the very ends, as if the tips have been dipped in ink. The fluffy feathers around her neck look softer than a cloud. I marvel at the precise origami of her folded wings and her strange, twitchy elegance.

Mira is mid-leap when she spots the bird. She wobbles ever so slightly and then crumples to the floor.

Anastasia scurries into the corner farthest from the window, dragging Mira with her. At the same time, Father charges forward, but Pritnip pulls him back. Krupnik goes to the window and greets the bird with a solemn nod. Just as solemn, the bird nods back, then takes flight. Its wings hardly move. It slices its way, swift and sure, through the darkening sky.

"Calm yourself, Oblomov," says Krupnik.

"But it's—there's—that was a *bird*!" splutters Father.

"Just as we observe them, they observe us," says Krupnik. "No doubt the Republic has heard there's a new director at the Center and is confirming your arrival."

Father is bright red; his cheeks are the same color as Pritnip's jacket. "And you tolerate this?" he splutters, looking from Pritnip to Krupnik, then back again.

"Things are . . . different here," says Krupnik. "We have an arrangement. A few of our balloons drift into the Republic. A few birds fly over the Center."

Father looks like he is about to explode.

Pritnip hurriedly says, "I expect you'll want to brief Oblomov and his family on how things stand with the Republic, Krupnik."

Krupnik nods and sits heavily in the nearest armchair. "The Republic is ruled by Ptashka III," he says. "She's a dangerous bird, if you ask me. Ruthless and clever, not to be crossed. The Republic has a strong military, but it's not strong enough to mount an attack on the Tsardom. And, like the Tsardom, the Republic keeps an eye on the other side, as you have just seen."

Pritnip nods. "There's been . . . shall we say . . . increased activity in the skies over the Center these last few days."

"Still," says Krupnik, "I have every reason to believe relations between the Republic and the Tsardom will stay just as they are. Peaceful, if tense."

"It's a strained kind of peace," says Pritnip with a wry laugh.

"But should anything happen to tip the balance in Ptashka's favor," says Krupnik, "I have no doubt she will seize her chance. The Republic won't be afraid of another war, Oblomov. Not if they think they can win it."

"But we're not in any danger, are we?" says Anastasia, still shrinking in the corner.

"Of course not," says Father. "At least we won't be for much longer. By the time I've put things in order around here, the birds will know exactly which side of the Stikhlos they belong on."

But no one responds to his confident statement.

The Krupniks leave soon after this exchange. Krupnik's grin grows even wider as he says goodbye, and I understand why he is so happy: He is leaving. Larisa hovers impatiently as we say farewell to them at the top of the ladder. They load the tarpans and start down the mountain. Krupnik turns and waves. Larisa doesn't give the Center so much as a backward glance.

CHAPTER FOUR

MUSHROOM SOUP

A welcome dinner has been arranged for our first evening by the ladies at the Beneficent Home. They meet us at their door, each of them older and more shriveled than the one before.

First is Glafira, whose bones make a clicking noise when she walks.

Next is Luda, as tiny and beautiful as a wrinkled porcelain doll.

Last is Varvara, wearing a black dress buttoned all the way to her chin. Her skin is so thin, I can see through it to the bones beneath. She must be at least a hundr—

"I am one hundred and fourteen years old, young lady," snaps Varvara. "What's more, I shall live for six days past my one-hundred-and-thirty-third birthday."

"Don't mind Varvara," Glafira says as she takes Varvara's elbow and steers her down the gloomy hall. "She's a voyant," she whispers over her shoulder to me. "But her gift has become . . . erratic lately."

A voyant? Is that some kind of yaga? I wonder.

"It is certainly not. A voyant is one who can read minds"—Varvara's voice drifts back down the hall—"and divine the future. Magic is not *my* purview."

We enter a dim room lit by grubby candles. In the center of the room is a table, and on it is a tureen with a moldy smell seeping from under its lid.

Luda presses Anastasia for the details of all the latest palace gossip. Father nods along while Glafira details her grievances about the various yagas to be found surrounding the Beneficent Home.

I remember the yaga we encountered on our sled journey, her face so close to mine, and I wonder if there are more of her kind in the woods below the Center. I suppose I could interrupt Glafira and ask, but then again, it won't do to seem too curious about yagas. I hold my tongue.

Varvara watches Mira and me intently and says nothing. I try not to think anything in particular in case Varvara overhears me.

At last, Glafira lifts the lid of the tureen and begins to ladle out the dinner.

At breakfast this morning in Stolitsa, before we were sent into exile, I ate salty cheese wrapped in crisp pastry along with beetroot soup, sharp yet sweet, and slices of fresh salmon as thin as tissue paper. The soup Glafira sloshes into my bowl looks like old bathwater.

"It's mushroom broth," Glafira says, and she points to the solitary mushroom floating on the liquid's surface.

I hurriedly slurp a spoonful. "Delicious," I say.

Mira sucks in her cheeks when a bowl is placed before her. Mira hates mushrooms.

Varvara turns to her. "I, too, detest mushrooms," she says.

Mira flushes.

"Unfortunately," says Luda, "mushrooms are the only things that grow in abundance here. They thrive in the damp. And until our next delivery of canned food—"

"Nasty, untrustworthy fungi," says Varvara. "Never popping up until your back is turned."

"I'm not very fond of radishes, either," offers Mira.

"Eat a radish!" exclaims Varvara. "You might just as soon eat an old shoe!"

Mira is eloquent on the subject of vegetables she can't tolerate. She and Varvara are soon absorbed in conversation. Luda is eager for more details of the goings-on at the palace, and Glafira has plenty more to say on the subject of pesky yagas. I stir my soup, catching snatches of the conversations that float around me.

". . . the ice sculptures were exquisite, of course, but they melted far more quickly than they have in previous years . . ."

". . . since the Magical Limitations Act, of course, yagas have been all but eradicated from most of the country . . ."

"Have you ever eaten broccoli, Mira? I never have, and I never shall!"

I am listening as Glafira explains to Father that the banya here is inhabited by a "most tiresome bannikha," when a creaky voice sounds in my ear.

"Tell me, Olga," says Varvara. "What did you do?"

"I'm not sure what you mean."

"What did you do to find yourselves here?"

"Don't you already know?" I ask.

"I am a voyant," she sniffs. "Occasionally I read thoughts. Occasionally I see into the future. But sometimes I need to rely on more traditional means of finding out what's going on. Conversation, for example. So tell me. What did you do to get sent into exile?"

I know very well why we have been exiled. The Sky Metro was Tsarina Yekaterina's pet project, an innovation that would have made her Tsardom the envy of the modern world. She wants Tsaretsvo to be a harmony of earth and air; she wants Stolitsa to be the City That Reaches the Sky. Some people say she is trying to conquer the birds with her Sky Metro and her zeppelins. I don't think anyone has been foolish enough to say it in her presence, mind you.

When the Sky Metro was complete, Stolitsa really would be the City That Reached the Sky. But it isn't complete, and Father is to blame.

I'm not close to Father. He thinks I am rude to Anastasia— *antagonistic* is the word he uses—and I think he's more interested in his scale drawings and architectural plans than his daughters. But I feel a rare tug of loyalty, and I say, "Father has been promoted."

"A promotion?" Varvara looks at me with pity. "A promotion to the Borderlands? Oh, no, my dear. Your Father has been exiled, and you along with him."

Glafira sets a platter of pickled mushrooms on the table. I spear one sharply with my fork.

"I don't mean to offend you," says Varvara. "Believe me, all of us here are being punished for something. See Glafira? She was more skilled at needlework than Yekaterina's mother, the Tsarina Agota. And Luda? Her offense was her face. She was, once upon a time, far too beautiful to last long in the court of someone as jealous as Agota."

"What about you?" I ask.

Varvara pauses. "My particular skills," she says at last, "are useful, but dangerous, too. I learned that quickly enough, not long after

I was sent to the Tsarish court as a gift from the king of Kyiv three days before my seventh birthday. Of course, in those days . . ."

I lean back in my chair. I'd better get comfortable. This story sounds like it's going to be long.

"Well, if that's how you feel, Olga," snaps Varvara, "allow me to tell you the abridged version."

I straighten up, and Varvara nods with approval.

"That's better," she says, and she continues. "One day, the tsarina asked me the whereabouts of—well, it's rather delicate. Let me just say she asked the whereabouts of something very important. And I wasn't able to give her the information she desired."

"Is that all?" I ask. "One mistake and Tsarina Agota banished you?"

"Oh, I was banished long before Agota's time. It was her mother who sent me into exile."

"Tsarina Pyotrovna?" I ask, and Varvara nods.

I think back to my history lessons. Pyotrovna was tsarina a hundred years ago; it was she who declared war on the birds.

"You've been here for an awfully long time, then," I say.

Varvara nods. "You'd think that after such an awfully long time, I'd be used to these mushrooms. But they still taste like slugs fished out of sewage, if you ask me."

Glafira glares at Varvara, but Varvara pretends that she hasn't noticed. She turns back to Mira and says, "You know, I'd rather be eating anything else, but what I would most enjoy is a slice of birthday cake . . ."

I push the rest of my pickled mushrooms away.

When Glafira brings dessert to the table, I worry she has found a way to include mushrooms in this dish, too. But it is a thin, goat-milk jelly, which tastes surprisingly good. I apply myself to my jelly.

By the time I have cleaned my bowl, the wind outside is so loud we have to shout over it to be heard.

". . . dancing was in the Ice Ballroom, of course . . ."

". . . and the ghosts in the trees are a terrible nuisance . . ."

"Tell me, have you ever had strawberry cake, Mira? I tried it once, and it was quite heavenly . . ."

There is a loud crack as the wind forces a window open. Outside, there is a swift, sharp sound, like knives slicing the sky.

Luda starts to scream, then stuffs her mouth with a napkin to muffle the sound.

It's birds. I hear them flying low, close to the roof of the Beneficent Home. Between the slice of wings, I sometimes catch a rattling, scratchy sort of sound. I wonder what it is—I can't quite place it.

"Claws," Varvara whispers. "It's their claws scrabbling at the roof."

The sound dissipates quickly. The birds are there, and then they are gone. I never even see them. Perhaps this should be a relief, but there is something unsettling about their sheer speed.

Father's face is very still. Mira's eyes are glazed with tears. She blinks them back.

Luda stands and bolts the window. "I'm sorry," she says. "It's silly of me to be frightened after all this time. And yet . . ." She shudders.

Father pushes his dish away. "Brazen creatures!" he says. "This cannot be allowed to go on." His voice is tense, almost angry.

The meal finishes in something very close to silence.

As soon as we're back at the Imperial Center for Avian Observation, Mira and I go straight to our bedroom. It is a small room that holds two narrow beds. There is a threadbare carpet on the floor and a circular window, like the porthole of a ship's cabin. I snuff the lamp—there's no electricity here—and we are plunged into darkness.

Mira falls asleep easily, and soon I can hear her snoring. Soft kitten snores. Even her snoring is sweet and charming.

I lie on my back, eyes wide open, staring at the roof. Is there a stalactite creeping through a crack in the ceiling? No wonder I'm so cold. I sit up and wrap myself tight in my blanket, and when I'm still not warmed, I take my coat from the back of a chair, beat the day's dust off it, and put it on. I give Mira a prod so that she rolls over and stops snoring, and then I climb back under the covers, where I continue staring at the ceiling.

I should be exhausted from the day's travel, but my thoughts are loud in my mind, and before one thought has even finished, the next has already begun: Who eats an onion raw like that?—white dogs with wet black noses—but am I glad to be here?—jingle-jangling diamond bracelets—pirouette, arabesque, who cares!—sent into exile—"Tell your fortune in a match!"

Enough!

I do the same thing I always do in Stolitsa when my mind won't rest at the end of the day: I put my hand under my pillow and pull out *Great Names in Tsarish Cartography.*

I light the lamp again, flip through the book, and settle on one of Londonov's last letters from the Unmappable Blank, dated March 1830 and recovered from the edge of the Blank in July 1831.

I have drawn the beginnings of a passable map, though I have lost three fingers to frostbite, which makes the work very difficult. I suspect I will lose one or two more before this expedition is complete . . .

Usually, half a page is all it takes for my eyes to feel heavy. But *usually* I read the book in my rose-wallpapered bedroom on the top floor of our apartment in Stolitsa. Here, it is different. Here, the tales of the Great Cartographers feel more real.

In the morning, after the sun rises and if the clouds are thin, I will see beyond the Low Stikhlos to the High Stikhlos through my bedroom window, the same mountain ranges Debrikov passes in chapter ten, the same peaks Londonov scales in chapter eight. I flip to the map at the front of the book: "Official Map of the Tsardom of Tsaretsvo and Environs." I trace my finger northwest of Kalinzhak, along the jagged line that marks the Low Stikhlos, to the spot where I think the Center must be, then farther north to the icy Northern Plains.

Cold shoots so sharply through my finger that I almost cry out. I pull my hand away and go to suck the pain from my finger—but it is already gone. I shake my head. I must have imagined it. It's been a long, strange day, after all.

I slam the book shut and toss it away from me. I snuff the lamp.

Across the room, the soft sound of Mira's snoring starts up once more. I stuff my head under my pillow to block the noise and wait for sleep.

Sleep doesn't come, of course. I remember the feeling of cold shooting through my finger so vividly it makes me shiver all over again.

Mira gives another dainty snore.

I think about waking her up to tell her what happened.

Mira would tell me I must have been dreaming. She would tell me that whether she believed it to be true or not.

Because if it really happened, if I wasn't dreaming, if the map really did come alive beneath my hand—well, girls have been sent to Bleak Steppe for less.

Yagas have been unwelcome in Tsaretsvo since the War in the Skies. After all, it was the yagas of the Imperial Coven at the Stone Palace who stole the firebird's egg. *Glorious Victory: An Impartial Account of the War in the Skies* says as much at the end of chapter three:

> *Once it became clear that the Imperial Coven had deceived her, Tsarina Pyotrovna wasted no time banning all yagas from the Tsardom. For the next three days, the roads out of Tsaretsvo were clogged with yagas. They rode bareback on horses and tarpans, they bundled into sleighs, or they simply told their shabby huts to pick up their chicken feet and scratch their way northward. No more than a week after the Coven stole the egg, every last yaga, every final scrap of magic, was gone from Tsaretsvo forevermore—and allow the authors of this book to be the first to say, good riddance!*

But it doesn't matter that Tsarina Pyotrovna banished all the yagas in the Tsardom by imperial decree—there's nothing the Stone Palace can do to stop girls from being born yagas.

Everyone knows this.

And everyone is watchful.

It starts around the time a girl steps into that strange space between being a child and being a woman. Around the time she makes her debut at the Spring Blossom Ball.

Perhaps she is good at guessing what tomorrow's weather will be. Too good. Perhaps she listens to the singing of crickets or the croaking of toads as if she understands what they are saying. Perhaps she sees shapes in the leaves at the bottom of her teacup. If she's out of the ordinary, strange in any way, then she might be a yaga.

She might not be one, of course. But better send her to Bleak Steppe, just to be sure.

The Bleak Steppe Finishing School for Girls of Unusual Ability is, like Father's recent promotion, a polite fiction. Everyone knows exactly why girls are sent there. When I was younger, we whispered about it every time there was an empty seat at assembly, every time one of the older girls disappeared. And then I got older, and we whispered about the girls in our class who suddenly disappeared: Katia, who walked into a swarm of bees and came out the other side without being stung; Zenia, who could multiply numbers like 1774 and 3965 without pausing to think; Polina, who saw strange visions in her inkwell.

Girls who are sent to Bleak Steppe have their hands cut off so they can never work magic with them again. They have their tongues cut out so they can't say any kind of spell. They're tossed into boiling water, and their bones are used for soup.

We never knew if those stories about Bleak Steppe were true. Because none of the girls who were sent to Bleak Steppe ever came back to tell us.

I huddle into my blanket. It is cold in here. Cold enough that you could trick yourself into thinking the cold was coming through the pages of a book. Still, I decide I won't tell Mira what happened. Nearly thirteen is a dangerous age, an age when it is best to keep anything strange—even if it *is* only something you imagined— to yourself.

I close my eyes, determined to sleep. Tomorrow, this will feel like nothing more than a dream.

When I wake the next morning, Mira is already up. She is looking out the window and twisting her hair around her little finger. I swing my feet onto the chilly floor and join her. The windowpane is covered with blooms of frost. Beyond the frost, the sky stretches wide and far.

"Did you know that you snore?" I say, and I sling an arm around her shoulders. But when Mira looks up at me, her face is pinched and anxious.

I stop my teasing.

"Wasn't it dreadful last night?" she says, returning her eyes to the window.

Wasn't what dreadful? I can't remember anything especially awful about last night, unless you count Glafira's mushroom soup. My tongue curls at the memory of it.

"We learned about the War in the Skies last winter," Mira says. I realize she is talking about the birds. "Madame Nazdrilev told us all about the horrible birds. Pecking peasants' eyes out. Catching children in their claws and carrying them off, past the horizon. Puncturing military balloons. And all because they don't want to share the skies." She shivers. "Cruel creatures."

"I'm sure our soldiers were cruel, too," I say lightly.

"There's just so much sky here." She presses her hand to the window. "In Stolitsa, there was never this much space."

"Aren't you forgetting the Glorious Victory?" I say. "Or did Madame Nazdrilev not get to that part? We won, you know. The war's been over for a hundred years. The birds leave us in peace, and we do the same to them."

"Well, what if they don't leave us in peace?" she asks, stubbornly refusing to be comforted.

I pull her close to me. "I won't let anything happen to you," I tell her.

She presses against me, then asks in a muffled voice, "Do I actually snore, Olga?"

"Yes, you actually do," I say. My stomach gurgles. "Coming for breakfast?"

She thinks. "As long as it's not mushrooms," she says.

The kitchen is even colder than our bedroom.

"There's nothing to eat here except mushrooms!" Anastasia's words come out in a cloud of steam. She flings herself into a chair in just the same way she did in *Three Blood Moons* when she read the portentous telegram. Only in *Three Blood Moons*, one of the chair legs didn't snap under her weight.

"Mushrooms!" she spits, picking herself up off the floor. "Nothing but *mushrooms*!"

"Let me look," I say, and I go to the pantry. I suspect the situation isn't as dramatic as Anastasia is making out—situations are rarely as dramatic as Anastasia makes out.

The shelves hold thick layers of dust, a collection of dead spiders, and . . . mushrooms. For once, Anastasia isn't exaggerating.

I get down on my knees and look into the pantry's darkest corners, where I find a sack of grain. I haul it out. Anastasia peers inside. "Millet," she says as a cloud of tiny, paper-winged insects flies out.

"Moth-infested millet," I correct her.

"I suppose it's better than mushrooms," mutters Mira.

Moth-millet porridge it is.

Mira cracks kindling, and Anastasia uses it to light the stove. I stir the porridge. Father comes downstairs and gets in the way, offering advice like, "A pyramid shape is best if you want the fire to catch quickly, darling," and, "If you stir from the elbow, Olga, you'll find the porridge won't clump together." It's annoying, I suppose, but he seems cheerier than he was yesterday.

Mira screws up her face at her first mouthful. "Why does it taste so dusty?"

Anastasia scowls.

"Do you think the dusty taste comes from the moths?" Mira asks.

Anastasia scowls harder, and this time Mira gets the message. She takes a theatrically large spoonful. "*Mmm*," she says. "Delicious."

The only person who eats with enthusiasm is Father. Having successfully supervised the porridge-making, he turns his attention to improvements to the Center.

"Krupnik has certainly let things deteriorate," he says through a millety mouthful. "Swarms of birds flying through the Borderlands with no repercussions. Frankly, I'm not surprised the tsarina sent me in."

His spoon clatters against his empty bowl.

I swallow a heavy mouthful. "More millet?" I say, offering the pan of congealing porridge remains.

He shakes his head and scrapes his chair back. "No time, I'm afraid. I have work to do."

"So do I," announces Anastasia. "My memoir is hardly going to write itself. At least here there's nothing to distract me from working on my life story."

Mira and I look at each other. When Anastasia works on her memoir, she likes to enlist at least one of us to take dictation as she tells rambling anecdotes about dancing with Rudolph Valentino or how Boris Lavrov made her a present of her white mink coat.

"Look at my nails!" I say, and I hold up my grimy hands to show Anastasia the dirt embedded beneath my fingernails and in the creases of my knuckles. "I need to wash. Didn't Glafira say there was a banya behind the Beneficent Home?"

"I'll join you," says Mira, gathering the bowls from the table. "I'm filthy after that tarpan ride."

"Be careful of the bannikha," calls Anastasia. "Glafira said that—"

But we have already left the kitchen and started down the ladder.

CHAPTER FIVE

MASHA THE BANNIKHA

I s that it, do you think?" asks Mira.

We are looking at a small, windowless hut set on the shale slope behind the Beneficent Home for Retired Ladies-in-Waiting. I can't think of what else it could be, and it doesn't look so different from the banyas I have seen in pictures, though there's no welcoming curl of steam rising from its chimney.

"That's it," I say, and I creak the door open.

We step into a small room. Its wooden walls are stained nearly black with smoke. Three of the four walls are lined with benches. The last wall is taken up by a large cast-iron stove and a bundle of rags. In one corner is a water barrel with a neat stack of silver dishes balanced on its lid. There's a row of hooks behind the door.

"The hooks must be for our clothes," says Mira, taking off her jacket.

It's cold in here. I make straight for the stove. "I suppose we need to light this," I say.

Mira pries the bottom compartment of the stove open and gropes around inside. Her fingers come away black with charcoal. "There's some kindling here already," she says, "but it wouldn't hurt to have some more." She crouches over the pile of rags, looking for something to burn.

The bundle of rags stirs, yawns, then straightens up into a creature about half my size. She has long, spindly fingers, soap-colored hair, and murky eyes.

Mira topples back into me, and I topple back into the stove.

"I'm sorry!" Mira gasps. "I didn't mean to . . . I mean, I didn't know . . . that there was a . . . a . . ."

The creature bows very low. "I am pleased to be at your service," she says. "I am Masha."

We look at Masha blankly.

"The bannikha," she explains.

"Oh," says Mira. "I see." Except her voice goes up at the end of the sentence, so it sounds like she doesn't see at all.

"New to this, are you?" asks Masha. "Let me explain. The rules of the banya are simple. You're never to enter it backward, or walk around it clockwise, or utter the numbers"—here she holds up her fingers to make first a three, then a seven—"or any multiples thereof. Neither are you to bring any coins inside. Gold, silver, bone—doesn't matter. I shan't tolerate them. You'll be provided with plentiful steam, hot and cold water, and such protections from evil charms and spells as it falls within my power to provide. Is that clear?"

Mira and I exchange glances. I don't think it's any clearer to her than it is to me, but Masha doesn't seem to mind. "Good," she says, and she ladles water from the barrel in the corner into two of the silver dishes. She places one in my hands and the other in Mira's. "Rinse!" she snaps.

We undress and douse ourselves with the water. It's so cold that I yelp as it prickles down my scalp and over my shoulders. I think of our bathroom in Stolitsa. It had a deep pink marble tub with gold taps, and you had only to turn them for plentiful piping-hot water.

While I am contemplating the benefits of modern plumbing, Masha bustles around the stove, setting a fire in its belly. Then she clears her throat, leans down, and makes a low, growling sound. When she opens her mouth, a bright tongue of flame shoots out and sets the kindling ablaze.

Mira clutches my arm. I drop my dish, and it clatters to the floor.

Masha straightens up and dabs her mouth with a corner of her ragged skirt. She turns around and catches us staring. "You two—"

she starts, but the words come out in a cloud of ash. She waves it away and tries again. "You two are acting like you've never seen a bannikha before," she says.

"The thing is," ventures Mira, "we haven't."

"We . . . we're not even sure what, exactly, a bannikha is," I admit. "Are you . . . are you some kind of yaga?"

Masha laughs. Or I think she laughs. Another cloud of ash escapes her mouth. "I'm not a yaga, sad to say," she says. "A bannikha is a bathhouse spirit—what magic we have is confined to steam and water and soap."

I am relieved Masha isn't a yaga, but perhaps a little disappointed, too.

"But you *are* magic," I press.

"You've really not met a bannikha before?" she says.

"I'm sure I never have," says Mira in her primmest voice.

Masha sighs, and a single cinder falls from her lips. "A silly question, really," she says. "Why should you have? Our days were numbered after the yagas were banished. No kind of magic was welcome in Tsaretsvo after that, no matter how poor or how harmless. One day I was stoking the stove in the Imperial Banya, and the next . . ."

She shrugs, fetches a dustpan and brush from the corner, and sweeps up all the ash and embers she has exhaled. Then she splashes a ladle of water onto the stovetop. The water sizzles as it hits the hot iron and turns into warm, fragrant steam. Soon the room is filled with it. I forget that just a few minutes ago I was shivering with cold, and I am soon quite convinced I will be warm forever. Mira and I sit on a low pine bench and let the steam wrap around us like a blanket.

Masha brings two more dishes of water and a ball of soap, from which she carefully unpeels a sliver. "Be sparing with it," she instructs. "Soap isn't easy to come by."

She sits and watches while we scrub the backs of our knees and between our toes. "Still," she says after a long time, "it's hard to imagine Stolitsa without any magic at all. Is it dull?"

"If you ask me, it's extremely dull," I say. "But I never knew it with magic."

"What was it like before?" asks Mira.

Masha is silent for a moment—but only a moment. And when she starts to talk, she doesn't stop.

She tells us about the green-haired water spirits who lived under the bridge in the Mikhailovsky Canal and sang to people as they crossed over it, and the blue-haired water spirits who splashed all summer long in the fountain in Tsentr Square. She tells us about the large, solemn birds that perched on the branches of the trees in the palace orchard, and the smaller, daintier birds that nested in the eaves of the Mariinsky Theatre and swooped down to pull open the velvet curtains at the beginning of every act.

She pauses to ladle more water onto the stovetop. It sizzles, and fresh steam, sharply hot, ribbons through the banya's warm fug.

She tells us about the street corner yagas who used to pick their way down the streets of Stolitsa in their chicken-legged huts, dispensing love charms and curses, and the Imperial Coven, who performed powerful spells for the tsarina. She tells us about the Imperial Banya—the most lavish banya you could ever imagine—with clouds of steam as white as snow and more than a hundred bannikhi carrying frothing dishes of soapy water to all the nobles who came to soak there.

"It sounds lovely," I say. "I wish I could have seen it."

"Well, I disagree," says Mira in a tight voice. "There's no reason to get all dreamy over yagas, Olga." She looks at me through narrowed eyes, and I know just what this look means: Girls have been sent to Bleak Steppe for less.

I think of the cold I felt through the map, and I shiver all over again. But I just shrug like I don't know what Mira is talking about.

She turns her shoulder to me and snaps, "Don't forget, it was the yagas who stole the firebird's egg. It was the yagas who started the War in the Skies." She wrings out her wet hair. "I think it was very wicked of them to take the egg for themselves."

"Well," says Masha, "it didn't happen exactly like that." She pours more water onto the stovetop and waits for the sizzle to subside. "Fire is dangerous, you know. A bellyful is more than enough."

"What does that mean?" I ask.

"It means that from the moment Golovnin brought back the firebird's egg, things changed. I know—a small, quiet bannikha can overhear a lot of interesting talk in the banya if she cares to. The birds worried that the tsarina wanted the egg for herself. The firebird, once it hatched, could be tamed and trained. Now, training the bird wasn't easy—unless you were a yaga, that is. But a trained firebird could be a powerful weapon. The tsarina already had fleets of balloons. With a firebird at her command, she could take over the skies. And the humans worried equally that the birds might take the egg."

"Is that why the Imperial Coven took the egg?" I ask.

"The yagas wanted to keep it safely away from birds and humans alike," says Masha.

"I find that hard to believe," says Mira in her most teacher's-pet-like voice. "Yagas are evil, deceitful creatures." I stop working my washcloth over my shoulders. A trickle of soapy water runs down the back of my neck. It *is* hard to think of yagas keeping something safe.

"I assume you've never met a yaga," Masha says to Mira. "The yagas I met in the Imperial Banya were kind and clever. And I don't doubt they meant to safeguard the egg. Not that it helped. It wasn't the egg that started the War in the Skies. It was the *idea* of the egg. From the moment it arrived in the Stone Palace, there was plotting and planning. I heard it all in the banya. If you ask me, Golovnin should have left it alone."

She sniffs. "I was happy in the Imperial Banya. Then, a squabble over a silly egg, a bit of sky, put an end to it all," she says. "And creatures like me suffered the most. Sent to the very edge of the Tsardom—some even farther. I expect there are hardly any of us left at all now." She blinks hard, like she is holding back tears.

Mira takes one of Masha's long, spindly hands in hers and presses it tight. Masha cheers up a little.

"Still," she says, "I hardly like to think of the state of the banyas in Stolitsa now that the bannikhi are gone. I expect their chimneys are stopped up and their corners are thick with cobwebs. I'm sure their stoves hardly sizzle at all."

"Actually—" Mira begins, but I talk over her.

"They're in a terrible state," I say loudly and firmly. "Dusty and dirty and generally falling to pieces." There's no reason for Masha to know that modern plumbing has come to Stolitsa.

Masha smiles to herself. "I suspected as much," she says.

CHAPTER SIX

SPINNING THE GLOBE

We leave the banya in a cloud of steam, pink-cheeked and scrubbed clean. As we walk back to the Center, we see a party of Pritnip's soldiers walking through the forest, rifles slung over their shoulders.

We reach the ladder that leads to the Center, and Mira springs nimbly up it. Two rungs from the top, she stops, and I stop below her.

A gust of wind wobbles the ladder, and my stomach wobbles, too. I try not to think about how far from the ground I am. "I'm sure you have an excellent reason for stopping," I say to Mira through clenched teeth, but she only looks down at me and presses a finger to her lips.

"Listen," she hisses.

All I can hear is the creak of the ladder. But then, over the creaking, I make out Anastasia's voice coming from above.

"The rumor that I sprinkled poisoned sugar on Anna Brenko's cherry dumplings is laughably false," she says. "Nevertheless, Madame Brenko did become suddenly and inexplicably ill on opening night. It fell to me, her humble understudy, to play the role of Antonia in *Symphony on the Moon*. The critics were unanimous: That night, a shining star was born!"

I roll my eyes. Anastasia has never understood that memoir-writing is supposed to be a silent undertaking.

We climb the rest of the way up the ladder and creep into the kitchen so she won't enlist us to take down her ramblings. Here we find Father and Colonel Pritnip deep in conversation, their heads bent over a map on the kitchen table.

Seeing the map is enough to set my nerves on edge.

The best thing to do, I think, is to stay far away from it. But even as I'm thinking that very thought, I'm walking toward the map.

The next-best thing to do, I tell myself, is not to touch it. But I am already reaching out a finger to the edge of the map.

"We shall extend our surveillance in a northeasterly direction," Father is saying, and Pritnip is nodding in agreement. I brush my hand across the map, and my fingers fall over the Borderlands. I don't feel anything under my hand. No sharp cold, no prickling ice. Nothing except paper.

I am relieved, in an empty way. Now I know that the coldness of last night really was just a dream.

But then a strange taste rises in the back of my throat. The taste of earth, tangy and mineral. I try to swallow it away, but it grows stronger.

"Olga," says Father, "what do you think you're doing?"

I pull my hand away. The taste disappears.

"I'm sorry," I say. "I didn't mean to interrupt."

Father looks at me and knits his brows. "You're pale," he says. "Are you feeling unwell?"

I run my tongue over my teeth to make sure the taste is gone. "I'm fine," I say. "A little tired."

"I'm a little tired," I tell Mira later when she asks why I keep staring into space while we play a game of cards in front of the fire.

"I'm a little tired," I say again when Anastasia asks why I'm not eating my bowl of stewed mushrooms.

But when I do go to bed, I can't sleep.

Great Names in Tsarish Cartography, with all its maps, is under my pillow. I can feel it there. I slip my hand under the pillow, and my fingers brush against the book's spine.

I know it's not natural to *feel* maps. To *taste* maps. But if I can keep it secret, no one need ever find out, and I won't be sent to Bleak Steppe. I just need to be careful, that's all. I take the book from under my pillow and stuff it between the mattress and the bedsprings.

But sleep still doesn't come, and now my fingers keep inching toward the mattress's edge.

I push back the covers and get out of bed.

The house is still and silent. Everyone is sleeping. I pace back and forth in the parlor for a while, but the parlor is too small for me to pace up and down in any satisfying kind of way. So I climb the ladder up to the observation deck, where I can look through the glass at the rippling mountains and the dark sky. It makes a much better backdrop for someone anxiously wondering if she might be sent to Bleak Steppe.

It's a clear night. The sky is dusted with stars, and an almost-full moon glints off the periscope and the curved surface of the globe in the corner.

The globe!

As soon as I notice it, I feel a thrill of unbidden excitement.

Then reason sets in. Don't touch it, I think to myself. You are plain, unexceptional, utterly normal, Olga Oblomova. And you'd better stay that way.

But reason is nothing against the magnetic pull of the globe. I reach out with just the very tips of my fingers, and I spin it. Continents and oceans blur together. It's hypnotic. When they finally still, I let my hand fall on a glossy patch of painted blue. The Squalid Sea.

But instead of touching the smooth surface of the globe, my fingers plunge into water. I feel the cold swish of the sea. So cold it makes the hairs on my arm stand on end. I look down as a wave of salty water gushes from the globe and sloshes onto the floor of the observation deck.

I know I should do something, but I stay where I am. Fixed to the floor. Standing in briny water that's halfway up my shins now. Water pours out of the globe, wave after wave after wave. In a corner of the room, I spot a bright school of fish.

The water is licking at my waist, but I don't pull my hand from the globe. I feel electric. Like I've unlocked a hidden door and I'm about to step through into something wonderful.

In the corner of my eye I sense a flickering movement. I whip my head around, all my excitement turning to dread. I am waiting to be discovered. But there is no one there.

No—wait.

There is something outside the window. A bird on the sill, squat and dark. It watches me with a small beady eye.

I let my hand drop from the globe. The water shrinks back and disappears. The floor is dry. I am dry. There's not even a salt crystal left on my fingers.

The bird opens its wings and flies off into the night.

What did it see? Why was it here?

I lean against the window. I feel ill. All the energy that coursed through me is gone, and I am left with only the terrifying certainty that I am—that I *must* be—a yaga.

I come away from the window. No one else must find out. I must avoid the globe. I must keep my distance from maps. As for *Great Names in Tsarish Cartography* . . . I bite my lip. I need to get rid of it.

I creep down the ladder and back into the bedroom. I ease *Great Names in Tsarish Cartography* out from under the mattress. I go to the kitchen and start to build a fire in the stove.

I am still sitting by the kitchen stove when Mira walks in, yawning.

"I didn't hear you get up," she says. "I normally do, you know. You're not what Madame Tansevat would call light-footed."

I didn't get up because I've been up all night. But I don't tell Mira this. Instead, I tear a page from *Great Names in Tsarish Cartography* and force myself to feed it to the stove.

"Olga!" Mira cries, and rushes forward. "What are you doing? Your favorite book!"

She grabs *Great Names in Tsarish Cartography* out of my tired hands.

"I'm sick of reading it! I want to burn the whole thing," I say.

"No, you don't," she says, and she gives it back to me.

I sigh. She's right. I could never give up Golovnin's map of the Infinite Steppe, Karelin's sketch of the Dezhdy, the sad story of Boris Londonov and his failed expedition into the Unmappable Blank. I've been trying all night to throw the book into the fire, but I just can't make myself do it.

"You're very strange this morning, Olga," she says.

"No, I'm not," I say firmly. "There's nothing strange about me."

Mira studies me with a look of confusion, but the look quickly passes. Soon she is bright and smiling again, and she gives my shoulder a squeeze before she lugs the pot onto the stove for our breakfast porridge.

Later, we are sitting at the breakfast table with Anastasia and Father. Anastasia is comparing her tarnished teaspoon unfavorably to the silverware we left behind in Stolitsa, and I am doing my best to ignore her, when a large gray bird glides past, swooping close to the window. There is menace in the slow, deliberate way it flies.

Father topples his chair in his rush to get to the window, but the bird is gone. "Well," he blusters. "I wonder what that display was in aid of. Ptashka's sending me a message, I've no doubt. Trying to intimidate me."

Pritnip is sent for, and in no time, he and Father are sitting at the table. The breakfast dishes lie untouched between them as they discuss the problem of the birds. Father is frowning and shaking his head. More than once, he smooths his moustache.

He notices me in the corner watching and shoos me away. He closes the door, but if I stand close outside, I can still hear everything they say.

"The egg is hidden in the Unmappable Blank—and not even Londonov himself could find his way out of the Unmappable Blank, much less find something hidden inside it," says Pritnip.

"But if everything I've heard is true, a trained firebird is a weapon far more powerful than an army's worth of guns and cannons," says Father. "A firebird can burn an entire village into nothing with one blast of its fiery breath. If it shook a feather loose, it could singe half a city out of existence"—I hear the snapping of fingers—"just like that!"

"Indeed," says Pritnip.

There is a long silence.

When Father speaks again, his voice is changed. He sounds almost excited. "Think," he says, "what a victory it would be if we had the egg for ourselves."

I slink away and into the parlor, back to Anastasia and Mira. I don't want to hear any more.

A few minutes later, the door slams, and Pritnip storms past us.

Mira twists her hair around her finger. "Why is Pritnip so angry?" she asks.

"I'm sure it's nothing," says Anastasia.

But it can't be nothing, because outside we hear him shouting orders at his men. Soon, the sky is filled with military balloons, far more balloons than I've ever seen. Father comes out into the parlor and stares at the balloons through the window.

"Aleksei?" says Anastasia.

He turns with a broad smile on his face and says, "Start packing your bags, my dear. If this venture is successful, well . . ." He adjusts his top button. "I expect it won't be long until I'm reinstated as head architect for the Sky Metro."

"Why, that's wonderful!" cries Anastasia at the same time as I say, "What venture?"

Father turns back to the window. The balloons are floating away from the Center, heading east. "I've commanded Pritnip to set up a military camp here, beneath the Center. They have mounted a preliminary expedition into the Unmappable Blank," he says. "To retrieve the firebird's egg."

My stomach drops. Anastasia's smile wavers. Even Mira, who is ten years old and hardly well versed in the intricacies of bird-human conflict, looks unconvinced.

But Father strides out of the room and up to the observation deck before anyone can question him.

From the day Golovnin brought the firebird's egg to court, relations between the tsarina and the Avian Counsel grew tense. At first, they argued over who rightfully owned the egg. Their quarrel grew—they could not agree on the division of land and sky, on the tsarina's use of military balloons, on who should control the clouds.

It's hard to say who attacked first; there are reports of swarms of birds in the North making raids on Tsarina Pyotrovna's military camps. There are reports, too, that one of Pyotrovna's military balloons flew too low over the Cloud Palace and damaged one of its turrets. Aggressions such as these became commonplace. It was perhaps inevitable that after a particularly bitter argument between Tsarina Pyotrovna and Ptashka I, head of the Avian Counsel, the alliance between birds and humans was formally broken and war was officially declared.

—*Glorious Victory: An Impartial Account of the War in the Skies* by I. P. Pavlova, chapter eleven: "The Battle Begins."

CHAPTER SEVEN

A BAG
FILLED WITH
MEMORIES

It has been seven days since we arrived at the Center. Six days since Mira and I met Masha in the bannikha. Five days since Pritnip's soldiers were stationed here on Father's orders.

In the kitchen, I make the porridge. As I stir, I look through the window at the mountainside and the forest.

Or what's left of the forest. Half of the trees have been cleared on Father's orders to make way for the military camp. Now the slope is dotted with tents. The silk envelopes of military balloons are spread over the ground. They'll be inflated as soon as the sun breaks through the clouds. Soldiers move between tents, warming their hands over campfires, passing tin cups of tea and tin dishes of shaving water, fastening their red jackets.

A thick, gloopy noise breaks me out of my thoughts. The porridge has bubbled over and is splattering the wall behind the stove.

"Olga, pay attention!" says Anastasia. "Breakfast is spoiling."

I take the pot off the stove and slop the porridge into bowls. From the communications room, the *beep–tick–beep* of the telegram machine sounds.

The telegram is still warm when Father, puffed up with pride, brings it to the table.

"Read it, Aleksei!" presses Anastasia.

Father reads:

TSARINA YEKATERINA CHARGES ME TO COMMEND YOU ON EXCELLENT PROGRESS IN INITIATING THE HUNT FOR THE FIREBIRD'S EGG STOP HER IMPERIAL HIGHNESS IS MOST PLEASED BY REPORTS OF YOUR DECISIVE ACTION STOP RESPECTFULLY YOURS IMPERIAL UNDERSECRETARY IVAN DEMENTIEVICH

"Wonderful," cries Anastasia, "just wonderful!"

Wonderful, I think, doling out the bowls of porridge.

Father finishes his in seconds, then scrapes back his chair and hurries out. I can hear him barking orders before he's even reached the bottom of the ladder.

Anastasia snatches up the telegram and reads it again. "Excellent progress," she murmurs. "Most pleased." And then she looks up sharply. "Do you know what this means?" she asks. "A commendation from Tsarina Yekaterina?"

Mira and I stare at her.

"It means," she explains, "that we'll be back in Stolitsa before we know it! I won't have to give up my part in *The Ghost in the Lantern* after all! And Olga—Olga will go to the Spring Blossom Ball!"

She dips her hand into her pocket for her gold appointment book and rifles through the pages. "Three weeks!" she gasps. "The Spring Blossom Ball is in three weeks! How can we possibly be ready in time? Olga, you will give over your days to deportment and grooming. You must study the steps of the mazurka and pore over your etiquette books."

I think I am supposed to be excited at this prospect, but I can't manage more than a limp shrug. I can't believe I'll have to be a Spring Blossom after all.

Anastasia flashes me a dazzling smile. "I've just had the most wonderful idea," she says. "Why don't we pay a visit to the ladies at the Beneficent Home? I can't think of a more pleasant way to pass the morning!"

There is something ominous in Anastasia's sudden enthusiasm, but I know there is no point in objecting when Anastasia speaks like this.

When we arrive at the Beneficent Home for Retired Ladies-in-Waiting, Varvara opens the door. "Well," she says when she sees Anastasia, Mira, and me on her doorstep, "this is a pleasant surprise."

A surprise? I thought Varvara could see the future. Some voyant she is, I think, and Varvara gives me such a narrow-eyed glare that I resolve not to think anything else for the rest of the visit. When she is finished glaring, she invites us in.

Before Varvara has time to pour the tea, Luda, Glafira, and Anastasia withdraw into another room and shut the door behind them. Mira and I sit across the parlor table from Varvara in awkward silence.

"It's nice weather we're having," Mira ventures.

"Nice?" Varvara's eyes flick over the sludgy windowsill.

"I mean interesting," says Mira desperately. "Don't you agree it's interesting to have snow so late in the season, Lady Varvara?"

"Hmm," says Varvara. "It is unusual, now that you mention it, to have so much snow at the start of April, even here in the Borderlands. Though I do remember a similarly snowy start to the month some years back—1863, I think it was, or '64 . . ."

From the folds of her dress, she produces a small velvet drawstring bag. She opens it carefully and dips her fingers inside. Her eyes go misty. "It was 1867," she says at last, "and the Neva was still frozen over at this time of year. The ice was thick enough to skate on all the way up to the first week of May." She takes her hand out of the bag. "Well, now, what are you two staring at? I suppose you've never seen a memory bag before?"

I shake my head.

"When you're as old as I am," she says, "you'll find you have more memories than you have room in your head to hold them all. Which is why I keep my memories—some of them, at least—in this bag. Memory bags are not easy to come by. You can't buy one off any old yaga. But with the right connections . . ." She coughs. "Here," she says, and pushes the bag across the table to us. "Why don't you try it? It's quite simple. Just put your fingers inside."

Mira dips a hand inside the bag. "Oh!" she gasps. "It's *wet*!"

"That's right, my dear," says Varvara. "Now move your fingers around, and you'll find a current of memory. Your surroundings will start to ripple around you as you enter the memory. Once there, you can walk around without anyone noticing you, but do be careful which doors you open—you can never know which memory will be waiting on the other side."

I look at Mira. Her eyes are just as misty as Varvara's were a minute ago.

"You try, too, Olga," Varvara says. So I pull my chair next to Mira's and dip my fingers into the velvet bag. They splash into an icy liquid that feels more like ink than water. I hear strange voices, as if two people are talking at one end of a long corridor and I am standing at the other.

"Wait," I say to Varvara. "How will I know how to get out?"

"It's easy enough," says Varvara. "Just look for the places where the memory starts to ripple around its edges—you'll see."

I hold my hand still in the cold pool of liquid. I hear more voices, not quite as far away now. I make out words, snatches of conversation, scraps of music. I taste fresh snow and slightly burnt toast and sweet, smoky tea. I smell the sharp tang of an orange just as it is sliced. Are these Varvara's memories? I look up at her, but it is like trying to see through water; the whole parlor is rippling and turning darker.

I start to feel ribbons of liquid flowing between my fingers, each moving in a slightly different direction. I grasp hold of one and feel it pull me inside. The memory comes to me in flashes: a bright gown, footsteps on a stone floor, a sudden cold in my bones. But then the memory spills open, growing wider and wider before me until it fills every corner of my vision, and I am not in the grubby parlor of the Beneficent Home anymore.

I am in the Stone Palace, in one of the reception halls, I'm sure. I've been in this room, or another high-ceilinged, gilt-wallpapered room just like it, at a Spring Blossom Ball rehearsal. A group of women stands around a ceramic stove, taking it in turns to press their backs against it and warm their fingers on its tiles.

Outside it is pelting rain. Every now and again, a crack of thunder rattles the windowpanes.

A woman with long blond hair takes the scratchy-looking fabric of her dress between her finger and thumb. "You'd think wool would at least keep us warm."

"I miss my silk gowns," sighs the woman next to her.

"Your gowns," snaps a stern-faced woman, "are being put to patriotic use. You know they're needed for patching the military balloons."

"I know." Another sigh. "But I still miss them."

The stern-faced woman snaps open a pocket watch. "Back to work," she says, making her voice loud over the rain, and the rest of the women peel themselves away from the stove and sit in a circle on the carpet. I creep to the edge of the circle. They are binding flint heads to arrow shafts.

"It's enough to make you miss embroidery," says the sighing woman.

All around the circle, the women are muttering to one another.

"Tsarina Pyotrovna doesn't know what she's doing," says one.

"She's rushed into this foolish war," says another, "without thinking of where it could lead."

"And the banishment of the yagas—it's outrageous! Where am I to get my love potions now that there are no yagas in Stolitsa?"

There is a loud crash, as loud as the thunder that has been rolling and cracking around the palace, but this sound is different. The sky is lit with yellow gun smoke. I hear a sharp cry. A body, silhouetted against the sky, falls to the ground. A balloon, punctured, follows. I suck my breath in as the falling figure hits the ground. I don't think I've ever seen anything so awful.

The women stiffen and pull their mouths down and go on with their work like they haven't heard anything. But their chatter has stopped.

So this is war. The same sort of war Father is in danger of starting, I think, with his search for the firebird's egg.

And then there is a loud shriek. The sky darkens. A flock of birds passes, strong wings beating the air. The women tense. They hold their arrowheads poised. Then the flock passes over, and the women pick up their conversation as lightly as picking up a dropped stitch.

"And don't get me started on the banya!"

"It's filthy without the bannikhi there. Simply filthy!"

But I can't stay as calm as the women. What if another body falls from the sky? What if it makes the same sick, thunking noise? I need to find the place where the memory ripples and turns wobbly so that I can leave.

Outside, another flock of birds flies past the window. I hear wild shrieking. I hear claws dragging over the roof. I run to the nearest door, fumble with the knob, and burst through.

And I find myself in . . . the same room. Exactly the same room, down to the gilt wallpaper. But now, the room is filled with women in bright gowns and men in evening dress. Birds perch on the chandelier and glide overhead. These birds don't have the same grim menace of the birds I've seen at the Center. They fly in crisscrossing patterns, like dancers in an elegant ballet. They make bright, chirruping sounds as they fly. They are wonderful to watch.

A band starts up with the *plink-plunk* of a balalaika. Some birds dip and soar in time to the music. People start to dance. This is a grand celebration.

In a corner next to the band, I sense a rippling movement—my way out of the memory. I walk toward it slowly, enjoying the feel of gowns swishing around me, the soft tickle as, every now and again, a feather floats against my cheek.

I am halfway across the room, when I see a group of three women standing apart from the rest of the crowd. One has scarlet-red hair. One is old, as crooked and knobbled as a tree bent over by the wind. One has a rain cloud hovering over her head. Rain falls around her, but she doesn't seem to be getting wet.

These women must be yagas.

I am drawn to them in the same magnetic way I was drawn to the globe on the Center's observation deck. I swallow hard. I don't want to be drawn to them.

I turn on my heel and rush to the place where the memory's edge is rippling, just to the left of the balalaika player. The scene starts to wash away, like when rain soaks the pages of a newspaper and all the headlines dribble together. Soon, the parlor of the Beneficent Home seeps into my peripheral vision. I ease my fingers out of the memory bag and blink a bit, and my eyes stop seeing everything in a wobbly, underwater way. Finally, the room falls back into focus.

Mira has taken her fingers out of the bag, too. "Was it really like that at the palace?" she asks Varvara. "Birds flying through the trees and singing such beautiful songs?"

Varvara nods. "For a time," she says.

"How wonderful," sighs Mira.

"What memory did you see, Mira?" I ask, suspecting it was not the same as mine.

"I was in the palace gardens," Mira says. "It was spring. The trees were in flower, and their branches were full of birds. And—oh, Olga, they were singing! It was like nothing I've ever heard before!"

I remember the shriek that ripped the air before the flock passed overhead in my memory.

"What did you see?" Mira asks me.

"Oh, nothing," I say. "Nothing so exciting."

Mira looks like she wants to know more, but I am saved by Anastasia's appearance in the doorway with Luda and Glafira. She is beaming.

"I have news," she announces.

Glafira looks at me, and then at Mira, and then at me again. With a sinking feeling, I know that she has compared the two of us and found me wanting. She lets out a low, heavy sigh and says, "It will be a challenge, Olga. But we are prepared to instruct you for the Spring Blossom Ball."

My heart drops.

Glafira shuffles closer, then looks me up and down once more. "I think it would be best," she says, "to begin immediately."

CHAPTER EIGHT
DANCING LESSONS

E very day, the balloons go up. Pritnip's soldiers head for the Unmappable Blank. Every evening, they come back empty-handed.

Pritnip tells Father that what he wants—to find the firebird's egg that the yagas hid in the Blank—is impossible. As soon as the balloons get near the Blank's edge, Pritnip explains, the navigational equipment stops working, and the snow falls so thickly that the soldiers can't see more than a few inches in front of their faces. It's only a matter of time before one of the balloons doesn't come back at all.

But Father doesn't listen. He is determined to find the egg and please the tsarina, no matter the cost.

So the balloons go up again and again and again.

Every day, too, brings a new telegram from the Stone Palace. Tsarina Yekaterina is most pleased with Father's efforts. Anastasia is so confident that Father will be back in favor and we will be brought back to Stolitsa in time for the Spring Blossom Ball that she has another one of her wonderful ideas.

A dress rehearsal.

Perhaps because there is so little in the way of entertainment here in the Borderlands, everyone except me thinks it's a wonderful idea. The ladies at the Beneficent Home brew nettle wine in preparation. Anastasia finds a somewhat flat area of ground on the mountainside that will serve as a dance floor. Pritnip and his men donate a torn parachute silk to our cause, and Glafira, the nimblest sewer, transforms it into a marquee.

The dress rehearsal is all anyone can talk about. Even the soldiers in their camp talk excitedly of the dancing and the wine—I overheard them on my way to the banya yesterday. I expect it will make a nice change from patrolling the freezing gray skies with their rifles cocked and ready or making dangerous forays to the edge of the Unmappable Blank. The soldiers always come back from the Blank with beards and moustaches icicled white from the cold, and more than one has lost a finger to frostbite. I suppose I can't blame them for welcoming the distraction that the dress rehearsal will bring.

I wish I could get as caught up in the bustle of preparations as everyone else. But all I can think about is what happens when I put my hand on a map. No matter how hard I try to stay away, I keep finding myself standing before the globe on the observation deck. And no matter how much I try to tell myself otherwise, I know I am a yaga, and I don't know how much longer I'll be able to hide it.

Never mind trying to become a graceful dancer, adept in the arts of polite conversation and fan fluttering for the Spring Blossom Ball. I need to work hard just to be a normal girl. The alternative is Bleak Steppe, and the thought of that terrifies me.

"One-two-three, hop, kick." I concentrate fiercely and chant under my breath, "One-two-three, hop, kick. One-two-three, hop, kick."

The dress rehearsal begins in five hours. I am dancing in the parlor of the Beneficent Home. Glafira sits in a corner, squeezing out a mazurka on a battered accordion. Mira sits next to her, tapping out the rhythm with one dainty pointed toe. Anastasia, Luda, and Varvara are on the lumpy sofa, watching me. I can't look up from my feet or I will lose track of the steps completely, but I can tell by Anastasia's tuts and Luda's small sighs that I am not impressing them.

"One-two-three—"

Gunshots drown out the accordion.

No one so much as flinches. "I never thought I'd get used to the sound of gunfire," says Luda, "but I've grown quite accustomed to it."

I am accustomed to it, too, but it disrupts my sense of rhythm. I lose my footing and hop-kick into the wall with a crash, and when I try to recover myself, I one-two-three-hop-kick into the mantel and knock a china shepherdess onto the floor.

Luda scoops up the decapitated figurine and smiles thinly. "Why don't we stop for tea?" she says.

The tea tastes like dust.

"That may be true," says Varvara, "but it's still not polite to say so."

"I didn't say so," I tell her. "I thought so."

"Ah," she says. "Sometimes I can't tell the difference."

Across the room, Glafira and Anastasia are talking softly, but not so softly that I can't hear them. "Of course, no one's going to be charmed by her posture," Glafira says, "but it's much improved since we began our lessons. And she recites 'The Clouds Were Stained with Blood' competently. The issue is—"

I can't see Anastasia's face, but I can tell by the tightness of her tone that it's arranged in a grimace. "You don't need to tell me," she says. "The poor child dances as if her legs were made of stone."

I scowl into my dusty tea. If Anastasia only knew—this stupid dance is the least of my worries.

Beside me, Mira is drumming the rhythm of the mazurka on the tabletop with her fingers. "You've got your thinking face on again, Olga," she says.

"I'm not thinking anything," I say. The words come out harder-sounding than I expected.

Across the table, Varvara fixes me with a shrewd look.

I take a deep breath, and when I speak again, the words come out more evenly. "If I am thinking anything," I say, "it's how stupid the mazurka is. Stupid and pointless. Like all dancing."

Mira pulls on a strand of her hair. "It's not stupid," she says. "Honestly, it's not. Let me show you—"

"I don't need you to show me," I say, but she has already pushed her chair back and moved into the middle of the room. She holds out her hands. I stay in my chair.

"Go on, Olga," says Luda eagerly. "Mira dances so beautifully. I'm sure she could help you."

Anastasia and Glafira are watching eagerly now, too.

I stand up and give Mira my hand.

"The steps are easy enough," she says. "One-two-three, hop, kick. One-two-three, hop, kick." She hops and kicks as light as air, and I follow along, hopping and kicking as light as rocks, but she smiles at me and just keeps dancing, so I keep hopping and kicking. And I do feel a little lighter—not as light as air, not as light as Mira, but lighter than before.

With a wheeze, Glafira starts the accordion, and then we are really dancing, in time to the music.

"Now comes the hard part," says Mira. "Forget the steps, and let the music carry you." Which is a truly nonsensical thing to say, and I am about to tell her so, but she smiles at me some more, and I think it can't hurt to try. So I stop counting the steps, and I listen to the music. I stumble at first, but when the music starts to sway left, I try to dance left. And when it sways right, I dance right. And when the music does a little hop, I do a little hop, and when the music does a little kick, I do a little kick. And when I look up and find Mira still smiling, I smile back. It feels good.

But the music doesn't carry me very far, and before long I can't hear which way to go or when to kick. I try counting under my breath again, but my feet turn heavy, and I stumble and collide with a side table, stubbing my toe on its leg. I double over from the unexpected pain of it. But the music doesn't stop, and when I straighten up, no one has even noticed that I've stopped dancing. They're all trans-fixed by Mira as she springs and leaps and kick-hops.

Mira hasn't noticed that I've stopped, either. She's immersed in the music.

It's not just her dancing that I'm jealous of, now. It's the ease of her; Mira makes the perfect Spring Blossom. I hate her in this moment, and I hate myself for hating her. She is perfect. And I am not.

I run from the room and from the Beneficent Home, letting the door slam behind me. I'm not wearing a coat, but I'm so hot with anger and shame that I barely notice the cold.

I am stomping through the trees, not even bothering to bend back their branches, just scraping my way through, when I hear pattering footsteps behind me.

"Olga!"

It's Mira. I suppose this means she stopped dancing and that when the applause subsided, she noticed I wasn't there.

I say nothing. I just walk faster.

"Olga! Wait!"

I am almost running now.

"Please, Olga!"

"What?" I say.

"I was only trying to help," she says meekly.

"Do you really want to help me?" I can hear my voice rising.

She nods. "Of course."

"Then disappear!" I'm yelling now. "Just disappear!"

I know how awful my words are, but I am too angry to care. I keep stomping back to the Center. I don't look behind me, but I can feel that Mira isn't following me anymore. She must still be standing in the trees where I left her.

CHAPTER NINE

THE DRESS REHEARSAL

I scramble up the ladder and make straight for the bedroom. I look at myself in the mirror. My face is pinched and blotchy from the wind. My hair is tangled. I sit and stare at my face. What kind of a sister am I?

Disappear, I told Mira, and I meant it. But I don't mean it now.

I am relieved when, at last, I hear her coming up the ladder. I find her in the parlor, doing relevés with one hand on the windowsill as if it were a ballet barre. She doesn't look up when I come in. She's stinging from my meanness. I'll apologize soon, and Mira will smile at me, even though I don't deserve her smile. Then everything will be normal again. This is the way it usually goes.

Right now, I need to focus on the Spring Blossom Ball rehearsal, on enduring all its small, painful humiliations while trying to look beautiful, trying to dance like I know how to do it.

I don't want Mira to disappear. Perhaps I want to disappear instead.

I go back to the bedroom, where a gown is laid out on my bed. I feel queasy. Turning myself into a Spring Blossom feels like an impossible task. Even with the right dress, with my hair brushed and my cheeks rouged, I'll still be me. A yaga. And if anyone finds out, I'll be sent straight to Bleak Steppe.

I reach for the gown, which is not my gown. Anastasia is the only person I know who would think it a good idea to take three traveling cases full of evening gowns to the remote mountains at the edge of the Republic of Birds. Three days ago, she made a great performance of giving me her green chiffon evening dress. "We can't all be practical," she said as she unpicked the seams to let out the sides of the gown. "There's no need to apologize for that."

"I wasn't apologizing—" I started.

"I'm just glad—pass me that pincushion, will you?— that one of us thought to be prepared."

Even with the seams let out as far as they'll go, the dress is very tight. But with Anastasia's opera coat—also bestowed upon me with a smug remark about sensible packing—over the top, the gown's too-tight fit is hardly noticeable. Well, hardly noticeable except when I have to sit or stand or draw breath or other minor things like that. Anastasia says that beauty is pain, but that makes no sense to me. Still, I will withstand the constricting gown for the next few hours.

Once I am dressed, I powder my face with Anastasia's compact and color my cheeks and lips with Anastasia's rouge. My hair is shining, and it falls in curls around my cheeks. I check my reflection in the compact mirror. My face is still the shape of a dinner plate, and my skin is still smattered with pimples. But even though I look exactly like myself, I do look just the tiniest bit nice. It's such a surprise that I smile. And I think that maybe this won't be so hard after all. Maybe I will dance passably and recite epic poetry passably and make conversation passably.

Maybe no one will ever suspect that I am a yaga.

Anastasia bursts into the room in a perfumed swirl of red silk and red lipstick, wrapped in the lavish folds of her mink. She looks so beautiful that my breath catches in my throat. "It's ten past seven!" she announces. "Our guests will arrive at any moment!"

She grabs my wrist, leads me out through the kitchen, and sends me down the ladder before I can say anything.

Outside it is sharply cold. Anastasia's opera coat is thin protection against the evening chill. A pale half-moon shines on the shale-flecked earth of the dance floor. It is eerily beautiful out here. I feel almost wistful. I wish I could be excited for the evening ahead. In Stolitsa, I scorned the idea of being a Spring Blossom, but now I wish more than anything that I was an ordinary Spring Blossom, concerned about getting her dance steps right instead of worrying about being packed off to Bleak Steppe. Though I *am* concerned about getting my dance steps right.

The ladies of the Beneficent Home are first to arrive, wearing ball gowns as ancient as they are.

"What a fine evening," says Luda while her fingers worry at the disintegrating lace of her collar.

Glafira looks me up and down. "You look quite acceptable, Olga," she says with a note of surprise.

I'm pleased with that. *Acceptable* is exactly how I hope to look, for more reasons than Glafira knows.

"But perhaps not for more reasons than I know," says Varvara in an ominous tone. She looks at me with unblinking eyes. A moth flutters out from between the folds of her skirt and flies into the cold twilight.

Does Varvara suspect that I'm a—I can't even allow myself to think the word in case she overhears it. And if she does suspect that I am the thing I can't even think, will she tell someone? Will she have me sent to Bleak Steppe?

"Now, Varvara, what did we say about telepathy?" says Luda brightly.

"That it'll spoil the ball," says Varvara with a sulk. "Which is actually untrue. The ball will go off very well even if Olga does trip three times in the mazurka and forgets part of the fifth stanza of 'The Clouds Were Stained with Blood.'"

Even in the middle of worrying that Varvara will tell everyone my terrible secret, I manage to be pleased that I will trip only three times during the dance.

"Although," adds Varvara, "the whole affair will finish in an abrupt and troubling manner."

Glafira sighs and steers Varvara over to the nettle wine.

"I won't tell," whispers Varvara over her shoulder as she walks past me.

Before I can feel any relief, Pritnip and his men arrive. They have polished their boots and waxed their moustaches. They all seem excited, even though some of them have bandaged heads and some sport slings around their arms. Father's search for the firebird's egg is to blame for their injuries, I'm sure.

As the air fills with the soldiers' conversations and the clinking of wineglasses, the dress rehearsal starts to feel like a proper occasion. We have a rugged, icy mountainside instead of the ornate, gold-leaf décor of the Stone Palace's reception hall,

Glafira on the balalaika instead of an orchestra, candles instead of chandeliers, and a murky brew of nettle wine instead of champagne. And yet the evening has a festive glow. If I wasn't the sole Spring Blossom, I think I would enjoy it. But I'm excruciatingly aware that I will shortly be called on to recite all seventeen stanzas of "The Clouds Were Stained with Blood." And even if I make it through my recital, there is still the embarrassment of the mazurka waiting for me.

Father clinks a spoon against his glass of nettle wine and opens the proceedings with a toast. Finally, he calls me to the stage, saying, "Our lovely Spring Blossom and my eldest daughter, Olga, will now delight us with an ode to the might of the glorious Tsarish military victory over the birds."

I recite "The Clouds Were Stained with Blood." I start off well, but I stumble in the fifth stanza. In the audience, Varvara nods knowingly. But Anastasia, behind her, mouths the words, and I keep going all the way to the end. My voice echoes off the mountains and hangs in the air in the moment after I finish and before the crowd's polite applause begins.

Now it is time for the dancing to begin. I swallow hard and tell myself it will be over soon.

Glafira plays the balalaika, and Pritnip partners me for the mazurka. It is not a success. At least not to start with. I can't find the beat, and more than once I feel Pritnip's toes crunch under the soles of my dancing shoes.

But then I remember what Mira taught me. I listen to the music and let my feet follow it. The steps come more easily, and there is something satisfying in the way my movements start to match up with Pritnip's. And, just as Varvara predicted, I trip only three times. When I finish, kicking my heel out with a flourish, I look for Mira's face in the small crowd to flash her a secret smile, but she is half-hidden behind the soldiers who are already coming forward for the next dance.

Glafira cracks her knuckles and applies herself once more to the balalaika. As the others begin to dance, I edge away. I pour myself a glass of nettle wine and take a mouthful. It burns my throat and sits in my stomach all heavy and scratchy, but it warms me. I sip slowly and watch the others take their partners.

Father dances with Anastasia. Her hair falls down her back, and his hand sinks into its thick mass. They are smiling into each other's eyes. Neither of them has looked happy like this, I realize, since we left Stolitsa. Pritnip spins Mira in circles. One of his soldiers waltzes Luda across the floor. Another soldier beckons to me, but I shake my head. I have had enough dancing.

I step away into the shadows and try to ignore how uncomfortable I am in Anastasia's tight gown. As I watch, the dancing becomes wilder and faster. Glafira strums furiously on the balalaika, and the soldiers on the dance floor keep pace, stamping and clapping and crying out for more. Father twirls Anastasia, and she spins out away from him, then back into his arms. Mira's skirt spreads out around her while she leaps and twirls. Her feet hardly touch the ground.

Then, suddenly, Glafira's fingers fall from the balalaika. A terrifying shrieking seems to come from every corner of the sky. I look up. There is a swarm of birds above us, and it is bearing down. The shrieking birds tear at the marquee with their beaks and claws. Silk splits and blows wildly in the wind created by their beating wings.

Wineglasses shatter, and there are screams as the dancers try to take cover.

I stand where I am. The birds move in a swirl that is disorienting and hypnotic. Looking at them turns my knees wobbly and makes my head spin. And then an arm—I don't know whose—reaches for me and pulls me under a table. My face is pressed against the ground. All I see are fragments of broken crockery and slimy puddles of uneaten mushrooms.

Then the shrieking subsides, and when I lift my head, I see Pritnip stand up from behind an overturned chair with his rifle cocked and aimed at the birds, who are high in the sky again.

In a rush of red silk, Anastasia tackles him to the ground. "Stop!" she screams. "Don't shoot!"

She points at the retreating swarm of birds. Inside their dark mass is something pale, slender, dandelion-haired.

Mira. They have taken Mira.

I only see her for a moment before the birds change direction. They fly farther and farther away, and then they disappear frighteningly fast. They were here, and now they are gone, and Mira is gone with them.

No one moves. A silence falls over us all. I can't seem to get up from the ground. Its cold seeps up and into my skin. I lie there blinking at the sky. It feels like we are under a spell.

Anastasia is the first to break it. She collapses into a dead faint. The fabric of her gown billows out around her, vivid red.

Then everything happens quickly. Father scoops Anastasia up and, grim-faced, carries her back to the Center. His lips are pressed very tightly together, like he is holding back a sob or a scream.

Luda helps me to my feet and brushes the dirt from my gown.

Pritnip springs into action, calling his men into a huddle. I hover at the edge of the tight knot of soldiers as they mutter about balloons and bullets and visibility. They brush me away, kindly but firmly, when I try to join in.

And then Glafira takes me by the hand and pulls me, protesting, back to the ladder that leads to the Center.

CHAPTER TEN

A SEARCH PARTY

I sit by the window and stare at the sky. It is so wide and black, so rippled with deep, dark clouds. I wonder where in this sky the birds have taken Mira. I will them to bring her back. She must feel so scared, so small, and so alone.

I don't sleep. I am sick with fear. And with guilt. I told Mira to disappear. And now she has.

Above me, I can hear the click of the telegram machine as Father tries to reach the Stone Palace. I hear his footsteps as he paces up and down, waiting for a response.

At first light, I see the soldiers assembling a search party below. I rush down the ladder.

Pritnip says that this is a military operation and that I must stay out of the way. I try to tell him that I don't care if it is a military operation or not—that Mira is *my* sister, and that it's *my* fault the birds have taken her. But all that comes out is a pained sob.

Pritnip softens. He allows me to hover at the edge of the search party and watch them if I promise not to interfere. I stand with my hands balled into fists and a lump in my throat.

The soldiers unpack a balloon envelope from a canvas bag. One holds a brass anemometer into the wind to test its speed. Another studies the sky through binoculars. I try to concentrate on the small details of these preparations: on the steam that comes from the nostrils of the tarpans; on the loop of braid that is starting to unravel from Pritnip's left epaulet; on the clicking sound the soldier's binoculars make each time they are adjusted; on the cold air biting at my face. I try to distract myself from thinking about Mira.

A soldier rattles a gas tank along the ground. The burner is lit, and the morning is torn open with heat and flame. The balloon's envelope fills and wobbles. Six grim-faced soldiers climb into the basket. Another whoosh of flame, and the balloon rises up. The soldiers on the ground loosen its ropes, and it floats away.

I want them to come back with Mira. I have never wanted anything more fiercely in all my life.

I watch the balloon grow smaller and smaller in the sky. I keep watching until it disappears from my view completely.

At last, I go inside and let sensation return, stinging, to my freezing hands and feet.

There's nothing to do now but wait.

Later that afternoon, the ladies from the Beneficent Home arrive at the top of the ladder. Anastasia emerges, pale and trembling, to receive them.

"Will you have some tea?" she asks, addressing no one in particular. The ladies all nod, and Anastasia disappears into the kitchen. A long time passes, and she doesn't return.

The ladies say nothing. Luda and Glafira sit and watch me with pitying eyes. Only Varvara looks calm.

The silence is almost too much to bear. I nod toward the kitchen and say, "I'd better help her." And I hurry out to the kitchen.

I find Anastasia bent over the stove, crying.

I've seen Anastasia cry before, of course. All of Tsaretsvo has. Sobbing prettily in *The Vanishing Maiden* when she woke one morning to discover she was slowly turning invisible. Wailing with abandon in *The Beast with Red Footprints* after the beast dragged her children out of the village and into the woods. Letting a single perfect tear roll down her cheek at the end of *The Seventeen Heartbreaks of Sofia Antonovna* as she turned and walked out the snow-dusted gates of the cemetery.

But I have never seen her cry like this. Her shoulders shake, and her hair is coming undone. Her face is blotched, and her nose is running. Anastasia—Anastasia Krasnoyarska, belle of Tsaretsvo's silver screen, one of the greatest beauties ever to be captured on celluloid—looks ugly. And for the first time, I realize I might love my stepmother.

I want to comfort her. But the longer I stand there, the more impossible it seems. And the harder she cries, the more I think that I might start to cry, too. And if I start to cry, I might never stop. I step around her instead. I fill the samovar with water and light the burner at its base.

I place the teapot on top of the samovar and carry it out to the ladies. Anastasia follows me. Glafira, Luda, and Varvara take turns offering words of sympathy and observations about the weather. Between these comments they leave pauses so long that the wind, howling outside, seems to be taking part in the conversation.

"Pritnip will certainly find her," says Glafira stoutly after the longest pause yet.

Varvara's eyes grow cloudy. "Pritnip won't find her," she says. "No one will find her until—"

"Oh, hush, Varvara," says Luda crossly. She lays her hand

over Anastasia's. "Almost none of Varvara's premonitions come true, dear."

But I remember the dress rehearsal. How did Varvara say it would end? *In an abrupt and troubling manner.*

"Until what?" I ask Varvara. "Until what?"

Varvara shakes herself, and her eyes turn clear. "I'm sorry, Olga dear," she says, "I must have dozed off there for a minute."

"Lady Varvara," I press. "You had a premonition. You said—"

"Look!" Anastasia stands so quickly her chair topples over. Outside the window, a balloon drifts to the ground. Father hurries down from the observation deck.

Pritnip's boots sound on the ladder, followed by his knock at the door.

He comes in and gives a small shake of his head. Anastasia drops her face into her hands, and Father makes a strangled noise and pulls at his collar. My eyes prickle with tears.

Soon the room is filled with red-jacketed soldiers. Pritnip unrolls a map across the table, and they crowd around it. I elbow my way between them until I can see the map, too.

The Tsardom is marked in green, the Republic in orange. Between them is a thin strip of yellow. The Borderlands.

Pritnip is pointing to the Borderlands.

"We were able to sail this far," he says. He moves his finger over the map, but it stays in the Borderlands and doesn't touch the Republic. "But then visibility became too poor. As for tomorrow, Oblomov has made some calculations."

Father clears his throat. "The barometer is giving a reading of one thousand and eleven. We can expect lighter cloud coverage tomorrow, so travel should be possible as far as the eastern sector of the Borderlands." He, like Pritnip, points to the strip of yellow. No one points to the orange part of the map.

"Why aren't you looking in the Republic?" I burst out. "That's where they've taken her!"

"A foray into the Republic," says Father, "without the express permission of the Stone Palace would constitute an unauthorized invasion and would frankly—"

"But that's where she is!"

He puts a hand on my shoulder. "This is a delicate political situation, Olga. I don't expect you to understand."

But I understand perfectly. "The birds have taken her beyond the Borderlands. They've taken her into the Republic," I say.

Father sighs heavily. "I've had a communication from the Stone Palace, Olga. The tsarina deeply regrets what has happened to Mira. But her orders are clear. We are not to enter the Republic. The search will continue tomorrow in the Borderlands, Pritnip," he says.

Then he leaves the room. I hear his feet on the rungs of the ladder to the observation deck.

The soldiers leave first, then the ladies, who wrap themselves in their shawls, ready to make their way back to the Beneficent Home. As Varvara passes me, she catches my wrist. "Here." She drops a small velvet pouch into my hand. It's her memory bag. My arm drops under the weight of it.

"Yes," she says. "It's heavier than it looks."

"What should I do with it?" I ask.

"It's a gift of sorts," she says. "You might find it useful."

After the ladies and Pritnip leave, Anastasia goes to bed. I go up to the observation deck. Father stands with his hands folded behind his back, looking out into the night.

"I want to find her, too, Olga," he says. "Just as much as you do."

"Then look for her," I say. "Look for her properly! Go into the Republic and—"

He whips around to face me, and in the half-moon's strange light, I see deep black hollows under his eyes.

"If it were that simple, Olga, don't you think I would? I can't risk sending Pritnip's men into the Republic."

"You've risked sending them into the Blank!" I say. "Why not the Republic?"

"If I were to send Pritnip and his men into the Republic, I'd be ordering a military invasion of a hostile territory. I'd be putting more than their lives in danger—I'd be putting the entire Tsardom in danger." He sighs heavily. "I'll find another way, Olga. We'll bring Mira back." He puts a comforting hand on my shoulder.

But I don't want to be comforted, and I shake him off. "You won't bring her back if you don't go looking for her," I say.

"The search party—" he starts.

"The search party is looking here." I point to the Borderlands. "But they've taken her here!" I forget for a moment that I am a yaga—that I need to conceal my strangeness. I place my hand on the orange-shaded patch of the map that shows the Republic, but instead of the map I feel frozen soil, and I gasp, both from the cold and the shock of what I have done. Wind whips around me like icy water. When I look to see if a window has come open, I find I am not in the Center for Avian Observation anymore.

An icy plain stretches out before me, dotted here and there with stunted trees. Wind tears across it—my clothes are thin protection against its bitterness. In the distance, the domes and turrets of a city are silhouetted against the sky. A pale sun glints off the golden tiles of the city's roofs. And then, over the rush of the wind, another sound: the familiar beating of wings. The air is thick with birds.

This is the Republic. This is where Mira is. I know it.

I pull my hand away from the map, and the room falls into focus around me once more. Father is staring at me openmouthed with a frightened, almost amazed look in his eyes.

I realize what I have done as Father's eyes narrow to blank, hard slits. He snatches the map away. "I never want to see such a display from you again, Olga. If you're smart—and I believe that you are—you'll understand how important that is."

He motions to the door, and I understand that I'm not wanted here anymore.

I sit on the edge of my bed, shifting Varvara's memory bag from one hand to the other. When the clouds part, the moon shines on Mira's bed. Her ballet shoes are tucked neatly under it. Her pillow still holds the dent of her head.

Mira is gone, and Father will not look for her.

I stand up and start to pace the room.

I stop my pacing. I start to lace my boots. And I decide.

I'm going to the Republic.

CHAPTER ELEVEN
ANASTASIA'S SNOW-WHITE MINK

I gather everything I think might be useful on a journey into the Republic. Two pairs of warm, clean socks. Gloves and a hat. And, because I can't bear to leave it behind, *Great Names in Tsarish Cartography*. I want to take the map Father and Pritnip had on the parlor table, the one that shows the Borderlands in detail and precisely plots the edge of the Republic. But Father took the map from me and placed it firmly under his arm. I look at the meager collection of possessions laid out on my bed. I suppose this is it, then. Along with a few jars of pickled mushrooms I'll pilfer from the kitchen, this is all I'm taking with me.

Next I need a bag. But the trunks we brought with us from Stolitsa are too large. I am considering improvising a rucksack out of an empty pillowcase when I remember Varvara's memory bag.

I weigh the memory bag in my hand. I am not sure this is exactly what Varvara had in mind when she gave it to me. I loosen its cord and peer inside. It does look surprisingly roomy. I start to fill it: socks, hat, and gloves in first, then the book. But as I place the book in the bag, my hand slips into the chill pool of Varvara's memories, and I feel the ribbons of liquid flow around my fingers. The dark bedroom turns watery around me, and I catch glimpses of bright, twinkling light coming from a chandelier. I hear the rustle of dresses and hushed conversation.

I am standing at the edge of a memory, but I don't have time to wander through it now. I need to leave for the Republic. But then, through the murmuring voices, I catch a sentence that makes me pause.

"Mark my words, the tsarina will be dangerous with a firebird on her side. There'll be nothing to stop her from taking control of the skies. *Our* skies."

The voice is coming from overhead. I look up and see two large dark birds perched on a rafter.

The second bird replies, "Which is why I put it to the Counsel that we must claim the egg for our own. The firebird is, after all, a bird. It belongs to us—it's one of us!"

The first bird dips its head in agreement. "Come," it says. "It's nearly time."

Time for what? I wonder as the birds swoop, one after the other, down the corridor, where a crowd of people and birds mills outside a closed door.

"I've heard it's the size of a man's head," says a woman close to me. The man beside her nods. "And as dark as a black diamond! Not long until we see for ourselves."

They're waiting to see the egg. The egg that started the War in the Skies.

The doorknob clicks and turns. I am drawn into the jostling crowd, and as the door opens, we all pile into a small chamber with brocade-patterned walls.

I can't see the egg at first. It must be behind the row of human guards, standing with their rifles shouldered, and bird guards, sharp-beaked and beady-eyed. I squeeze my way forward, past ladies in gowns and men in grand suits, and finally I see it.

It's no bigger than my own clenched fist, and its shell is a dusty charcoal-gray color. Even sitting on a gold satin cushion and surrounded by dozens of guards, it is underwhelming.

"It's smaller than I thought," grumbles a man with a long beard. "Can it really be the firebird's egg?"

"The tsarina is certainly hoping it is!" says the man beside him. "The question now is—"

But the crowd closes in, and I am pushed back away from the egg and don't hear anything more. Back in the corridor, I spot the thin, rippled edge of the memory, and I start to walk toward it, when I notice three women half-hidden behind a curtain. They are strangely familiar. One is young, with hair as shiny and red as an apple. The next is as old and wrecked-looking as a crumbling ancient monument. The last has hair as pale and crackling as a fork of lightning, and she smells powerfully of rain.

"If you ask me," says the young, beautiful one, "it's a lot of fuss over nothing. Let them squabble over it. We yagas have nothing to worry about."

Yagas! My breath catches, but I draw closer.

The crumbling old yaga frowns. "You may be seven hundred years younger than I, Anzhelika," she says, "but that doesn't excuse your silliness. It's what's *inside* the egg that should have you worried. If you ask me—" She tries to prod the younger yaga in the chest, but her finger falls off her hand.

My stomach curls, but the yagas don't seem concerned. "It's there on the carpet, Devora," says Anzhelika, pointing to the dropped finger.

Devora mutters to herself, and I watch in proper skin-crawling horror as tiny spiders scurry in dozens—in hundreds!—out of the folds of her skirt and across the carpet. They lift the finger up and carry it to Devora's outstretched hand, stitching it back into place with sticky cobwebs. The old yaga flexes her hand until she is satisfied it's attached.

"Devora's right," says the rain-smelling yaga. "You're too young to remember the firebirds—they can be dangerous in the wrong hands."

"Oh, Basha, you're overreacting." Anzhelika tosses her hair. "Firebird eggs take centuries to hatch."

"They take centuries to hatch," says Devora, "*unless—*"

"Hush!" snaps Basha. "Watch your words, Devora!"

"I don't see why I should hush," mutters Devora. "No one knows about the tail feather. And besides, none of us has a firebird's tail feather at hand."

Basha glares at her. "I think it's time we leave." She sweeps away, and the other two follow.

I watch them go. Could they be the Imperial Coven—the yagas who stole the firebird's egg?

I turn back to the place where Varvara's memory is wobbly and rippled. And I step through and into my bedroom once more.

I move quietly, careful not to wake anyone. But when I come into the kitchen for some jars of mushrooms, I find Anastasia is up. She stands over the table, holding a pair of silver scissors.

Their blades catch the lamplight. I cast around for some excuse to explain my appearance in the doorway fully dressed so late at night, but my mouth has other ideas. The words fall out before I can stop them.

"I'm going to the Republic of Birds," I say. "I'm not coming back without Mira."

My plan, put into words, seems suddenly impossible.

"I know," says Anastasia simply. "And it's very cold out there."

The scissor blades swish open. Anastasia shears a strip from—

"Your mink!" I gasp, and I gather up the snowy-white fur from the table.

"Well," she says as she cuts another strip away, "it wouldn't fit you as it was. You're hardly as slim as I am. But"—she straightens up—"this piece will make a good warm collar for you. This one can line your boots, and this your gloves. And there is enough left over for a hat."

"Why are you doing this?" I ask. "How did you know I would leave?"

Anastasia closes the scissors and puts them down on the table. "Before I was the most famous and best-loved actress Tsaretsvo has ever known—" She stops.

"Yes?" I prompt.

"Olga, can you keep a secret?"

I nod.

"Well, don't just nod!" she says. "Promise me you'll keep this secret."

"I promise," I say.

Anastasia inhales sharply. "This could ruin my reputation if it ever came out, you know. The truth is . . . the truth is, I wasn't raised by a herd of wild tarpans."

I cover my mouth with my hand to hide my reaction.

"I know this is shocking for you to hear, Olga," she continues. "But I'd never even seen a tarpan until Krupnik had me ride one. It was all just a story. A pretty story made up by Studio Kino-Otleechno to make me seem more exotic. The truth is that Anastasia Krasnoyarska, daughter of the wild horses, sounds infinitely more appealing than Olenka Kravchuk, daughter of the drunkest fisherman in Molodizhne. No one would buy tickets to see Olenka. Here, give me your coat, your boots, and your gloves."

I hand them over.

Anastasia holds a needle up to the lamp and expertly threads it. She sews the fur into the lining of my collar. "Olenka—that's me," she continues. "I was born Olenka Kravchuk in Molodizhne. Do you know Molodizhne?"

"No."

"The only reason anyone might—unless they had the bad luck to be born there—is if they stopped on the way to take the waters in Odets. As Boris Lavrov did the week before my fifteenth birthday. I lived, then, in a one-room wooden house. The sea rose over the floorboards when the moon was full and the tide was high. I went out fishing every day. My hands were thick with fish guts when Boris Lavrov spotted me by the side of the pier. When he leaned down from his carriage to speak to me, I shoved my hands into my pockets so he couldn't see them.

"The studio scrubbed the fish scales off me and taught me how to show my teeth when I smiled, how to walk in a gown without tripping over the damn thing, and"—she snaps her fingers—"I was a star."

"Well," I say at last, "there are no wild horses, but it's still quite a story."

"Not a happy story, though," she says. "Not entirely. Of course, I was glad to leave Molodizhne. But I had a little sister. Galina. I loved her. I still love her. And I left her behind, too. Like she was nothing. I don't know where she is now. But I know there's no gown so beautiful, no film role so glamorous that it could ever make me happier than I would be to see Galina again."

She hands back my clothes. I slip my arms into my coat and pull the collar around my neck. It is so soft and warm.

"I was selfish then. And, well, you certainly try my nerves from time to time, Olga, but if there's one thing you're not, it's selfish. You're a better sister than I ever was."

"So you won't stop me going into the Republic of Birds," I say.

Anastasia's eyebrows shoot up so far, they almost disappear into her hairline. "It's certain to be incredibly dangerous—all kinds of terrible things could happen to you! Just the thought of you going there is unspeakably awful—as awful as the thought that Mira might never come back." She finishes her sentence on a hiccupping sob.

"Then why?" I say.

She puts down the mink and looks into my eyes. "Could anything be more terrible than staying here while your sister is out there?"

No, I think to myself. Staying here would be unbearable. Impossible.

Through the window, the sky is still dark, but its blackness is fraying. If I don't leave now, it will be dawn, and Father and Pritnip will stop me from going.

"It won't be dark much longer," I say, and Anastasia nods.

"Come back soon," she says, handing me two jars of pickled mushrooms, a hurricane lamp, and the mink hat. "For my sake. You're both very dear to me, you and Mira. And for your Father's sake, too. He loves you both, you know."

I nod. I do know, though I don't always show it.

I button my coat, slip on my gloves, boots, and hat, and gather my bag. I say goodbye to Anastasia at the top of the ladder, and she wipes a tear from her eye. I don't know if she is crying for me, or for Mira, or for Galina. Perhaps she is crying for all three of us.

I climb down the ladder and go out into the dark.

CHAPTER TWELVE

THE FEATHER SMUGGLERS

I start down the mountain. The slope is slippery shale, made slipperier still by the scrim of ice coating it. I pick my way down in the wobbly pool of the light my hurricane lamp casts.

A rock gives way beneath my feet, and I break my fall with an outstretched hand. My palm smarts even through my glove, but I suck in my cheeks and keep going. In a way, I'm glad my path is so difficult. I can't think about anything other than where to place my feet.

I am halfway down the mountain when I notice the first glimmer of light. Can it be morning already? I'm exposed here on the bare side of the mountain. Even worse, the sky is clear, and the wind is calm. Conditions are perfect for ballooning.

I don't have a lot of time before Pritnip and his search party take to the sky.

The slope is threaded with thin veins of ice. I've spent most of my journey avoiding them, but now I seek one out and skid down it on my back, gathering speed as I go. When I reach the tree line, I connect feetfirst with the trunk of a tree and come to a crashing halt. I can already feel bruises forming, but there's no time to stop. The slope is thinly dotted with trees. I scramble down to where they grow closer together. When I am sure I'm well concealed, I look up at a patch of sky between the bristling fir branches.

I wait for what feels like a long time.

At last, a balloon floats into view, then another and another. There's a small fleet of them, almost motionless in the air.

They drift eastward, one after the other. I keep walking, staying safely out of sight. Soon enough, Father will discover that I am missing. Anastasia may be a talented actress, but she won't be able to cover for me for long. I scramble downhill, deeper and deeper into the shadows of the forest.

Spring comes late in the north. In Stolitsa, the ice over the Neva will have already broken into shrinking islands. The trees will be covered in buds and the beginnings of pale leaves. Here, the trees are bare, all except the firs with their thick cover of needles.

I keep one eye on the sun as I walk, using the direction of my shadow to steer my way north. This is a trick I learned from *Great Names in Tsarish Cartography*. Golovnin used it when he traversed the Golden Plain.

I begin to worry. There's nothing I want more than to find Mira and bring her home. But wanting something and being able to do it are two very different things.

Apart from the idea that I should head northward, I have no idea where I'm going. Not really.

I don't even have a scale map, save for the small maps in *Great Names in Tsarish Cartography*. Father made very sure last night to keep the large map out of my reach.

I should stop composing this dispiriting list of the challenges that lie before me, but I keep on.

Even if I do make it to the border of the Republic, it's highly likely that I, too, will be captured by the birds.

In fact, I'll be lucky if I'm captured by birds and not killed on sight.

If I do make it over the border and into the Republic of Birds and, by some happy accident, I find Mira, what then? It's not like I have a plan . . .

Stop it, I tell myself. Just stop it. I compose an alternate list in my head: Reasons Why This Expedition to the Republic of Birds Is the Best Option.

1. Mira is there.

2. Mira is there.

3. Mira is there.

4. Now that Father has uncovered my secret, it's only a matter of time before I azm sent to meet a dreadful fate at Bleak Steppe, so there is no reason not to go to the Republic.

5. Mira is there.

There. That's better. I go through the forest with a new sense of purpose. The snap of frost-brittled twigs under my boots feels good, and I settle into a steady rhythm. With each step, each snap, I am closer to Mira.

Then, out of nowhere, a clean, whistling sound shoots past me, somewhere near my left ear, followed by a sharp *thunk*. I realize the sound was made by the arrow currently pinning the left sleeve of my coat to the trunk of a birch tree. At first I am frozen with shock, but then instinct takes over. I try to wriggle out of my coat, but before I am free of the sleeve, another arrow whistles through the air. This one pins my right sleeve to the same tree, leaving me dangling like a puppet. My heart leaps into my mouth, and I watch with nauseated panic as a boy walks through the forest toward me. His bow is strung taut with another arrow, and this one is pointed at my chest.

"What have we here?" he asks, putting his pinched face very near to mine and bringing the arrow's sharp head so close that it almost touches the skin of my neck.

I swallow hard.

"An infiltrator," he says. "An obtruder. A creepsome, interloping prowler. The sort to stick her nose into things that are none of her business."

"I'm not an interloper," I protest weakly.

He lowers the arrow and nods at the plush mink collar of my coat. It's a stark contrast to the worn, leathery clothes he wears. "You don't expect me to believe you're from around here, do you? What kind of preposterousity is that?"

"Okay," I say. "I am an interloper. But not a sticking-my-nose-in-places-where-it-doesn't-belong kind of interloper. I'm just— I'm just passing through." I try not to sound too nervous.

"Well," he says, "you are powerfully blanched. White, that means—as white as paste."

"I have to confess, I've never been nearly stuck through with two arrows before. I'm feeling rather . . . rather . . ."—I search for exactly the right word before finishing triumphantly—"discombobulated."

"Discombobulated," he repeats, turning each syllable over on his tongue. He lowers the bow, plucks the arrow from it, and slots it into the quiver he wears over his shoulder. "What are you doing in the Between, then, if you're not sticking your nose into other people's business?"

"Where is the Between?" I ask. "Here?"

The boy nods.

"I'm looking for my sister," I say.

"And you think you'll find her here?" he asks.

"I think I'll find her north of here. In the Republic."

He looks at me warily, then braces himself against the birch and pulls the arrow from my left sleeve, then the other one from my right sleeve. "Come with me," he says, and he turns to go. "I can help you."

I stand there for a moment, wondering if I can trust someone with a quiver full of arrows and a sharp aim. But before I can decide, I realize the boy will disappear into the forest in a few steps, and I find myself running to catch up.

He leads me to a clearing where a man hunches over a small fire, poking at a meager pan of what smells like some kind of stew. Beside him is a grubby hessian sack half-full of something. The man looks up when he sees me and quickly pulls the sack closed.

"This is Fedor," says the boy, pointing at the man. "And I'm Fedor," he finishes, pointing at himself.

"People call me Big Fedor," says the man. "To avoid—"

"To avoid perplexity and suchlike," says Fedor. "And you are?" He gestures at me.

"I'm Olga," I say.

"What are you doing here, Olga?" says Big Fedor. He takes one look at my mink collar and makes the same assessment as Fedor. "You're not from around here. Although"—he wiggles a finger through the hole in my left sleeve—"it seems Fedor gave you a warm welcome. Not very hospitable of you, Fedor."

"She says she's looking for her sister—in the Republic, of all places," scoffs Fedor, and I can feel the blood rising in my cheeks.

Big Fedor draws the sack closer to him. "Something to eat, Olga?" he asks. "Breakfast's nearly ready." He nods at the bubbling pan.

Even though I've only been walking for a few hours, I am starving. And I want to find out how Fedor can help me. I don't have time to sit around a campfire, but my stomach betrays me with a thunderous rumble.

Big Fedor chuckles and pats the ground beside him. "I'll take that as a yes," he says.

I sit down cross-legged on the cold ground. Fedor hands me a bowl. We all eat quickly. The stew tastes as good as it smells; it is simple but warm and spicy, and I can feel it filling my empty stomach.

"And what about a cup of tea to finish?" asks Big Fedor. I nod gratefully.

He dips a hand into the sack and produces a battered kettle and three tin mugs. Something black and glossy and leaf-shaped floats out of the sack and hangs in the air for a moment before it falls very gently to the ground. I pick it up and stroke it through my fingers. "Is it a feather?" I cry.

"It seems you've found us out," says Big Fedor with a shrug.

"Took you long enough, too," says Fedor. "Not very perspicacious of you, I must say."

At the risk of sounding even less perspicacious, I venture, "Found out what?"

"We're feather smugglers," says Fedor proudly.

"It's an honest living," says Big Fedor. "Nearly honest."

"We hunt for feathers in the Between. And sometimes . . . a little farther than the Between."

"What do you do with them?" I ask.

"Sell them," says Fedor. He shakes the sack of feathers out onto the ground, and he and Big Fedor begin to sift through them. Fedor holds up a fluffy white feather. "Ones like these we sell for stuffing," he says. "For pillows and eiderdowns and the like. Ones like this"—he holds up a glossy blue feather—"we can sell for trimming. Feathers make very elegant trimmings for gowns and coats."

"No one in Tsaretsvo would dare wear feathers," I say. "Not after the War."

"There are plenty of French ladies will pay a high price for a feather from the Republic of Birds," says Big Fedor.

"Now"—Fedor seizes a long, iridescent feather in an emerald shade—"a particularly fine feather like this one could be used to decorate a hat." He runs it over his palm. "This is a particularly serendipitous find."

"This one's not," says Big Fedor bluntly, and he pokes at a dry brown feather with the toe of his boot and sends it floating through the air. "Worthless."

The feather falls on the ground before me. Fedor is right—no one would possibly pay money for it. It is the color of a dead leaf.

I draw the feather over my palm. Even though it looks brittle, it feels good: soft and fluffy and just a little greasy. I wonder where it came from. Could it have been dropped by one of the birds that snatched Mira? I think of her alone and scared in the Republic, and I remember that I have no time to waste.

"What can you tell me about the Republic?" I ask.

"Typical," spits Fedor. "All she wants to know about is the Republic. No one has a care for the Between. I don't like being inconsequentialized."

"I'm sorry!" I protest. "I just didn't know there was anything here—there's nothing marked on the map."

"The thing is," says Big Fedor, "the Between isn't just the border that divides one land from another. It's filled with people and creatures that don't really fit there"—he jerks his thumb toward the Republic—"and don't really fit there, either"—he jerks his thumb back in the direction of Tsaretsvo. "Do you see?"

"I see," I say. I think back to Stolitsa and my awkward attempts to fit in with the other Spring Blossoms. I think of the look that came into Father's eyes last night when my magic brought the map to life. "I see exactly."

"My grandparents came from the Northern Plains," Big Fedor continues. "The War in the Skies was bitter there. It was bitter most places, from what I hear, but the Northern Plains were hit the hardest. My grandparents took shelter in the Between, like so many others, and waited until they could return to their home. They had brought hardly anything with them. A few Azkabi carpets. A moonstone necklace. The family dictionary—as I'm sure you've noticed, young Fedor has a most prestigious vocabulary."

"A most *prodigious* vocabulary," corrects Fedor.

"But by the time the War was over," says Big Fedor, "the map had changed. And my grandparents' home didn't exist anymore."

"But a place can't just disappear, can it?" I ask.

"Oh, it's still there," says Big Fedor. "Only by all accounts, it's changed so much that it's a different place altogether. With a different name, too. The birds call the city Ptashkagrad now." He slurps the last of his tea. "Ptashkagrad's the capital of the Republic of Birds. That's where your sister will be."

Ptashkagrad. It must be named after Ptashka I, head of the Avian Counsel and leader of the Avian Army during the War in the Skies. "How do I get there?" I ask.

"Find the River Dezhdy," says Fedor.

"And how do I do that?" I ask.

"You'll know you're close when you reach the Dead Wood," says Fedor. "The Dezhdy flows through the middle of it." When he catches my expression, he explains, "It's not as terrible as it sounds. In the War in the Skies, most of the forest here was burned away. And for some reason, the Dead Wood never grew back. You'll come upon the Dezhdy if you go far enough into the wood, and then all you need to do is follow it upstream to its source, and the Republic will open out before you."

I nod. The source of the Dezhdy is in the High Stikhlos. And the Republic lies on the Stikhlos' other side.

I slurp the dregs of my tea and thank the feather smugglers. I know where I'm going, more or less. I have a full stomach. I feel almost optimistic.

I stand up to go and notice I am still holding the dull brown feather. "Here," I say as I hold it out to Fedor.

"Keep it if you like," he says. "We've no use for it."

I tuck it into Varvara's memory bag, and I bid the Fedors goodbye.

I haven't gone far when Fedor appears behind me.

"Here," he says, and he presses an arrow into my hand. "Take this. Not everyone in the Between is quite as hospitable as we are."

In the weeks after Golovnin returned to court with the firebird's egg, there was talk of little else, but one question intrigued everyone more than any other: When would the egg hatch? The court scholars searched the Old Stories. They were filled with tales of fierce, proud firebirds: birds that could singe whole cities with their fiery wings. Birds that lived for a thousand years before combusting in brilliant bursts of flame and cinders that left only ashen eggs behind, then hatching from those eggs anew. But the Old Stories said nothing about how the egg would hatch. The palace voyant was consulted, but her prediction—that the egg would not hatch for more than a hundred years—was dismissed as preposterous. The imperial horticulturalist tried potting the egg in rich soil in the conservatory as if it were a rare orchid that might be coaxed to bloom; the court alchemist tried his recipes on the egg, to no avail; Ptashka I, the head of the Avian Counsel, tried sitting on the egg three nights in a row in hopes that the warmth of her feathers would tempt it to hatch. Not a single crack appeared in the egg's charcoal shell.

Then the egg disappeared. It was taken in the night from under the watch of the armed guards who surrounded it. It did not take the tsarina long to deduce what had happened—after all, the egg wasn't the only thing missing. Her Imperial Coven had vanished, too. The palace voyant was once again consulted. The Coven, she said, had hidden the egg in the Unmappable Blank. The tsarina's once-trusted magical advisors had proven false and sly.

—*Glorious Victory: An Impartial Account of the War in the Skies* by I. P. Pavlova, chapter three: "The Deception of the Coven."

CHAPTER THIRTEEN

AN UNEXPECTED ENCOUNTER

The trees grow closer together. The forest grows darker. I keep walking, one foot in front of the other, toward the Dead Wood.

But soon the snap of twigs beneath my boots isn't the only snap I hear.

I stand very still and listen.

Snap . . . snap . . . snap.

I'm not the only thing moving through the trees.

Still, I tell myself, that's no reason to get spooked. All kinds of things live in a forest. I'm hardly going to let a few little faraway scuffling sounds stop me from finding Mira.

I set off again, walking in a brisk, unbothered way, swinging my arms to give a general appearance of nonchalance. And I nonchalantly curl my fingers tight around Fedor's arrow.

But the thing moving behind me—whatever type of thing it is—is a thing undeterred by my nonchalance. The faraway scuffling and snapping grow nearer. Louder.

I decide to try a different tactic. I'll turn around and wait until I see what's following me. I'll look at it coolly, assess whether or not it's a threat. Just like Londonov did on his expedition to the Bloodlands when he came upon a pack of red wolves. He stood statue-still and stared them down until one by one they whimpered away.

Yes. I'll do exactly as Londonov did. And whatever happens, I won't scream.

I stop and turn around.

I scream.

A yaga's hut is lurching toward me on its chicken legs, rustling leaves and branches as it goes. It hurries over to where I'm standing, then sinks to the ground. It seems expectant, like it's waiting for something. But I don't intend to find out what.

I pelt through the trees. I don't look back, but I can hear it behind me, crunching and snapping. I can feel it, too—the big, mossy bulk of it.

But what am I running from, exactly? Why am I running from a yaga's hut when I am a—

It still makes me feel faintly ill to admit it, but I *am* a yaga. And a yaga's hut is nothing to be afraid of, and neither is the yaga who lives inside.

I turn around. I can see the hut scurrying to catch up with me. My breathing is short and shallow. There's a difference between thinking there's nothing to be afraid of and actually not being afraid. I'll keep making for the Dead Wood, I tell myself. I'll just nod at the yaga's hut and keep going.

Maybe I'll even knock on the door. Maybe the yaga inside will be grandmotherly and full of wise and practical advice. Maybe—just maybe—walking up to a yaga's hut and knocking on its door is a good idea.

I tighten my grip on the arrow, just in case I'm wrong, and I head straight for the hut.

There's no smoke coming from the chimney. The roof tiles are thick with moss, and the window is dulled by a layer of grime.

The hut stands before me, its chicken feet curled neatly under itself.

Its door falls open. And before I can think about whether it's a good idea, I step inside.

· · ·

The hut is empty, dark, and musty, veiled with tattered cobwebs and thick dust. There is no yaga here. The most sinister thing I can find is a heap of old bones rattling around in the bottom of a copper pot, but I suspect these are the remains of some long-ago dinner.

I pick up a yellowed newspaper from beside the fireplace. It is dated 17 May 1824, and its headline reads: "Tsarina Pyotrovna and Avian Counsel in Deadlock over Hot Air Balloon Question." I think of Pritnip and his soldiers and the fleets of balloons they send up every day. The next report is titled: "Imperial Alchemist Claims, 'I Can Hatch Firebird's Egg.'"

Eighteen twenty-four. That's more than a hundred years ago. I feel strangely sad to think the hut has been empty that long. There's no yaga here. No one to give me advice or help me find Mira. I reach to open the door, go back into the forest, and continue my journey, but the hut lurches sideways. I'm tipped to the floor, tangled in chair legs. The hut lurches again.

Somehow, I find my feet and go to the window.

Of course. The hut is standing on its chicken feet. It bounces up and down on its legs in a way that feels more encouraging than violent, though a milk jug falls from a shelf and shatters on the floor.

The hut picks its way, unsteady yet swift, through the trees. We are covering a lot of ground, but we seem to be going in the wrong direction—away from the Dead Wood.

The hut makes a sharp turn. Now we are going in the right direction. I look out the grimy window. The trees blur together as the hut races past them. I give the wall a stroke. "Take me to Mira," I say, and the hut skips a little before it returns to its speedy stride.

When it is nearly dark, the hut slows, and it soon stops and sinks to the ground as if settling in for the night.

I try the door, but it won't budge. I'm stuck here, it seems, and I'm hungry. I poke through the shelves, looking for something to eat, and I find half a tin of tea and a jar of preserved cherries. I fill the samovar and brew some tea. It tastes of mildew more than anything else, but it is warming. The cherries are so sour they make my tongue curl, but, along with half a jar of pickled mushrooms, they will do for a meal.

Then I crawl under the cobwebbed blankets of the yaga's narrow bed, and in a moment I'm asleep.

CHAPTER FOURTEEN

THE HOUSE THROUGH THE MIST

I wake to the strangely comforting feeling of the bed rocking, and I sense the steady lope of the hut's chicken legs running again. I look out the window. The sky is still gray, and the forest is dark, but the trees outside are dead, black and burned. Their branches are jagged and bare, and the ground is ashen soil.

I must be in the Dead Wood.

I can almost feel the war that happened here so long ago. Death lingers between the blackened trees as if the ghosts of the dead soldiers inhabit the emptiness.

But in the middle of the Dead Wood is the River Dezhdy, which will lead me to the High Stikhlo Mountains, and on the other side of the High Stikhlo Mountains is the Republic of Birds—and Mira. Even now, I can see a grassy, sloping bank through the trees. The riverbank.

But the hut turns sharply. It pushes into a thicket of trees, out of the Dead Wood and into a patch of icy forest.

"You are going the wrong way, hut," I tell it firmly. "We must follow the river."

The hut continues into the forest.

I don't like being ignored. "Listen to me," I say. "You're going the wrong way. The Dezhdy leads up into the High Stikhlos, which lead to the Republic, which is where"—I feel my voice catch—"which is where Mira is."

The hut quickens its pace. Rain starts to spatter against the windowpanes. I start to shiver, and not just because the icy rain is leaking through the roof; I'm shivering because this creepy hut is taking me somewhere I don't want to go.

I go to the door, but it is still stuck.

I wrench the knob. Nothing.

I lean my whole body against the door and push with all my might. Still nothing, and even worse, the hut tips so that I lose my balance and crash against the opposite wall with such a thump that all the pots and pans clatter down from their hooks. I charge at the door with the arrow Fedor gave me, but the arrow splits in half on impact.

I try the window, but as soon as I have undone the latch, it relatches itself.

"I hate magic," I say. "And I hate yagas."

But if I hate yagas, I guess that means I hate myself. And why shouldn't I? It was hard enough to like myself when I was plain, ordinary, sometimes-spiteful, often-envious Olga. Stepdaughter of the beautiful Anastasia. Sister of the talented and charming Mira.

But now I'm not ordinary and unremarkable—I'm different. Different in the wrong way. I think of the look of fear and horror that came across Mira's face whenever we talked about yagas. And the shock on Father's face when he saw me enter the map the night I left the Center.

My nose is running, and I realize I am crying. I wipe the snot on my sleeve. See? Yagas really are disgusting. Then, because I'm not finished feeling angry, I pick up one of the pots that fell when the hut lurched and throw it against the wall as hard as I can.

The hut keeps running through the forest.

I slump against the wall and sink to the floor, disturbing a layer of dust in the process. It floats around me in a thick cloud, then settles. I don't know how long I stay there, watching the trees slide past the window while the rain falls more and more heavily and drips through the roof.

I am trapped, and I will stay trapped until the hut has taken me wherever it wants me to go. I don't know where that is. I only hope it's where Mira is.

The thought of her frightened and in danger makes me so desperate that I haul myself up again and start kicking at the door. I kick so hard that it splinters beneath my boot, even though I know it won't open for me.

But just as I give it one last kick, the door opens, and I hurtle through it, landing in a cold, murky puddle. The hut spits Varvara's memory bag out into the puddle, too, along with my hat, coat, and gloves.

I look up to see iron gates looming in the mist.

With a creak, they swing open.

I don't like this at all.

I gather my belongings and scramble to my feet and make to run, but an outstretched chicken claw prods me through the gates and onto a muddy path. I am about to turn and try to run again when I notice the house. It is tall and turreted, and its roof is studded with gargoyles. In books, enormous houses with foreboding iron gates and roofs studded with gargoyles often appear out of the mist—but not like this. This house is part of the mist, as if it is made from the weather.

Something about it holds me. I can't look away.

From somewhere behind me, a voice says, "Olga Oblomova, welcome."

I am already cold in a soaked-with-muddy-puddle-water kind of way, but hearing my name like that turns me another kind of cold altogether.

A woman appears beside me. She is small and round, with silver eyes and silver-white hair and a face as wrinkled as an old raisin. She holds a silver umbrella to protect her from the rain. I am struck with the unplaceable feeling that I have seen her before.

"How do you know my—?"

She steps around me and gives the hut a brisk pat. "Very well done, little hut," she says. "Thank you."

The hut dips down on its chicken legs, almost like it is curtsying, then scrabbles back into the forest.

The gates creak shut behind it. And I see the letters wrought in iron at the top of them. From where I stand, they are back to front, but it takes me barely a moment to work out what they say.

I feel the blood stop in my veins. They say:

BLEAK STEPPE FINISHING SCHOOL

FOR GIRLS OF UNUSUAL ABILITY

CHAPTER FIFTEEN

BLEAK STEPPE

I am standing inside the gates of the Bleak Steppe Finishing School for Girls of Unusual Ability. The school from which no girl has ever returned.

The school where girls are boiled down to their bones and their bones are boiled into soup.

I rattle the gates, but I know they won't open.

"You'd best come in," says the woman. My fingers are blue from the cold, but I cling to the gatepost. I will never find Mira now.

"There's nothing to be afraid of," the woman says. As she walks toward me, a chain of keys clanks around her neck.

I curl an arm around the gate. If you ask me, there's plenty to be afraid of. I remember all the whispered conversations between the girls at rehearsals for the Spring Blossom Ball about the things that happen to the girls who are sent to Bleak Steppe. Sent *here*.

"You needn't be frightened," she says.

I don't move.

"You know," she continues, "girls come here with the strangest ideas in their heads. They beg us to spare their hands, plead for us not to cut out their tongues. They scream wildly that they don't want to be thrown into the soup pot. Those rumors aren't true, Olga. Why would we want to drain the magic out of young yagas when we are yagas ourselves?"

I keep my grip on the gate, but I turn my head just the tiniest amount so that I can see her. "You mean . . . you're a yaga?"

The woman takes a key off her chain. She tosses it onto the ground. It winks brightly before it is sucked under the mud. Am I supposed to be impressed?

The woman watches the ground intently. She smiles when the soil starts to bubble and a mound of dirt forms. "Stand back," she says, and before I can ask why, a slender tree has sprouted from the ground. It grows quickly. It is soon as tall as I am, then twice as tall. And it is shining silver. Its branches spread out, leaves unfurl, blos-soms appear, and finally, heavy silver orbs grow from its boughs: apples. A tall silver apple tree stands in the place where the key fell. It is beautiful and eerie in the misty night. I could gaze at it for hours.

"More of a showy trick than practical magic," says the woman, "but it illustrates my point. Now, will you come inside?"

I stay where I am. Wind ruffles the branches of the tree. A silver apple falls to the ground.

"Of course, you can always stay where you are, hugging the gatepost. But I think you'll be happier inside." She wraps her hand around the tree trunk and gives it a twist, and the tree disappears. When she opens her hand, the key rests on her palm. She threads it back onto its chain and walks toward the misty house.

"Pick up that apple, won't you?" she calls from farther down the path. "They can be surprisingly tasty."

I pick up the apple, slip it into my bag, and follow her down the path, trying to ignore the fast, loud thump of my heart.

We come to the most enormous door I have ever seen—and I have seen the front doors of the Stone Palace. The doorknob is set as high as my head, and the strange—yet also strangely familiar—woman has to stand on tiptoe to reach it. She heaves the door open. And with a feeling of sick inevitability, I follow her through to meet my fate.

The inside of Bleak Steppe is not at all like the outside. We stand in a cavernous hall of blue-tinged stone. It is warm in here, thanks to the blazing fire that crackles blue in the center of the room. My clothes and boots, which were soaked from the mist and caked with mud moments ago, are now dry and clean. I touch my hair and then my face. They are dry, too. Noise floats down from upstairs. It takes me a moment to work out that it is the patter of footsteps. Chatter. Laughter. *Girls'* laughter.

The woman walks briskly across the floor. "There'll be plenty of time for gaping later, Olga," she says, and I realize my mouth is hanging open. "The dining hall is this way."

We go through another door and pass a small room filled with buckets of soapy water where dirty bowls and dishes appear to be washing themselves—they jump into the steaming water, tangle around with the dishcloth, then leap out again, flicking themselves dry in the process.

The woman clears her throat. "What did I say about gaping?" she says.

I scuttle after her and come out into a long, narrow room occupied by a long, narrow table. All the seats around it are empty, but it is strewn with crumbs and stray forks and spoons, and there is a pile of dishes at one end. It seems the school is full of girls. Real, live girls who haven't been turned into soup.

"I expect you're hungry," the woman says, and she looks up at the ceiling. "Baba Basha, Olga has arrived."

The blue-tinged stone of the ceiling ripples and darkens. Clouds roll across it, growing thicker, turning gray, then darkening until they are almost black. A clap of thunder shakes the walls of the room, and the clouds break apart. It's strange and beautiful to watch, though I don't understand what it has to do with me being hungry. I don't understand much about Bleak Steppe at all.

"Watch out, Olga," the woman says, smiling, "or you'll get splashed."

Rain falls from the roof. And it is only because I have seen a series of similarly impossible things—a key that turns into an apple tree, a fire that burns blue, a kitchen where the dishes wash themselves—that I do as she says. I stand back as if I am quite used to rain falling from the ceiling, and I watch as it pools on the table-top. Only it doesn't pool; it falls into the shape of a bowl of dump-lings and a plate of biscuits and a cup of tea, a hunk of bread, a wedge of cheese, and half an onion.

Then the clouds above us roll away, and the rain stops. But the food remains. It looks and smells quite real, and apparently it tastes quite real, too, because the woman bites into the cheese with satisfaction.

"How—?" I start, but she waves me away.

"Eat first. Then there'll be time for questions," she says through her cheesy mouthful.

The dumplings are delicious, rich and good and spiked with

sharp herbs. Next I eat the biscuits, the whole plateful, and slowly lick the crystals of sugar from my lips. Then I slurp the tea down in one swallow.

Across the table, the woman takes alternating mouthfuls of cheese and bread until she finishes both. Finally, she turns to the onion. She sprinkles it with salt and raises it to her lips. And then I remember. The sled. The snow. The paper twist of salt. The muttered conversation with the yaga in her hut.

"You're the onion woman!" I cry. "From the sled!"

"Onion woman?" she says with a crunch. "That's hardly flattering. My name is Mijska. Baba Mijska to you."

"I can hardly believe it," I say. "You must admit it's quite a coincidence, us happening to take the same sled."

She fixes me with a shrewd look and bites into her onion. "I'll admit no such thing," she says when at last she is finished chewing. "When it comes to our pupils, we leave nothing to chance. It's easy to get some of you here. Others present more of a challenge. But we make sure you all get here eventually. You don't really think it was a coincidence that I sat next to you on that sled?"

"But why—?" I begin.

Mijska cuts me off. "Because Bleak Steppe is the only place where you are free to be what you are."

I have so many questions that I want to ask. Is Bleak Steppe really a school? What does it teach? How do you know that I'm a yaga? Have you been watching me this whole time?

I must look bewildered, because Mijska swallows the last of her onion in one quick gulp. "Perhaps I'd better start at the beginning," she says.

The beginning of what, I wonder.

"Bleak Steppe was founded nearly one hundred years ago," Mijska says, "by Baba Basha, one of three members of the Imperial Coven—"

"The Imperial Coven? The yagas who stole the firebird's egg? The ones who started the War in the Skies?" I say, barely believing this could be true. And haven't I heard the name Basha before?

Baba Mijska frowns. "That's a history lesson you'd do well to unlearn, Olga. The Coven didn't *steal* the egg; they *concealed* it. And if they hadn't, the War would have been much worse. Better a divided Tsardom than no Tsardom at all."

I nod, but I'm still not sure I understand her. After all, a yaga *would* say that the Coven was only hiding the egg. Then again, Masha said the same thing in the banya back at the Center for Avian Observation. And if the stories about girls being boiled down to their bones at Bleak Steppe are not true, then perhaps the stories about the Coven might be wrong, too. I press my hands to my temples. My head is beginning to hurt.

"They paid a high price, though," Baba Mijska continues. "And the rest of us paid it along with them. Once the yagas were banished from Stolitsa by the tsarina, the Tsarish people were quick to turn against us. Many of us left Tsaretsvo. Most went to places where their particular skills were welcomed: the Argentinian pampas, New York, Tasmania. I hear there's a large number of Tsarish yagas living in the Bermuda Triangle. But some stayed. A lot of the older, more traditional yagas couldn't be persuaded to leave. They took to their huts and wandered the Borderlands instead, plying their magic. But even yagas can't live forever. Most of the huts are empty now, though they're not without their uses."

"Like carrying girls to Bleak Steppe against their will?"

"Well, you were hardly going to come voluntarily, were you? Not with all those terrible rumors. You know, Bleak Steppe is the only school of its kind, the only one that instructs yagas in the art and science of magic. You are a yaga, Olga, and Bleak Steppe is where you will learn your craft."

"And what is that?" I am leaning forward. My fingers grip the edge of my chair. "What is my craft?" I can hear the delight in my voice. I am hungry to know. All of a sudden, I can't think of anything more wonderful than being a yaga.

"The better question would be," she says, "what is your medium? A yaga's medium is the one thing she can bend to her will. Or I should say, the one thing she can learn to bend to her will."

"What's your medium?" I ask.

She takes my teaspoon and stretches it out into a long silver ribbon. "I should have thought it was obvious," she says, and, tying the ribbon into a bow, she turns it into a spoon once more. "It's silver. But yours will be something quite different. It might be wax, or oak wood, or silk, or sugar."

"How do I find out what it is?"

Mijska covers the teaspoon with her hands, and when she opens them again, the spoon has turned to a silvery liquid. The silver runs through her fingers and spreads slowly over the table until it is a shiny pool, almost like a mirror. I look into it, and Tsaretsvo appears in outline across the silver. Lakes and forests and mountains and cities appear. On the corner, a compass rose shows north and south, east and west. The silver has formed a map.

"Maps," I say, almost laughing. It makes sense. *I* make sense. "My medium is maps!"

"Hmm, most useful," says Mijska thoughtfully. "You will start tomorrow."

"But, Baba Mijska," I say, "I can't. I must go. My sister—"

"Mira," she says, and I look up in surprise—how could she know about Mira?

"Well, we are yagas, dear," she says, and then she presses my hand in hers. "A most precarious situation. You will have to learn fast."

CHAPTER SIXTEEN

A GLIMPSE OF PTASHKAGRAD

I stare at the empty plate in front of me, trying to make sense of things. Bleak Steppe is a school where girls who are yagas learn their craft. Girls like me. I am brimming with excitement. But then I remember: I don't have time to learn—I need to find Mira.

Then again, maybe Baba Mijska can teach me to use my medium to help me find her. I push the plate away. "Baba Mijska," I say. "Whatever I need to learn, I need to learn it tonight. I must set out for the Republic tomorrow."

"I see you're anxious to leave," says Mijska, "but I'm afraid that won't be possible. No girl leaves Bleak Steppe before Baba Basha decides they may."

"Baba Basha is here?" I say. "Baba Basha of the Imperial Coven?" I remember now—I've seen her in Varvara's memories.

"Baba Basha is headmistress of Bleak Steppe and, yes, one of Tsarina Pyotrovna's Imperial Coven," says Mijska. "You can't go until she feels you're ready."

I stand, scraping back my chair. I don't care what Baba Basha feels—*I* feel ready to leave right now. "Take me to see her," I say. "She'll understand why I need to leave. I know she will!"

"Baba Basha *is* very understanding," says Mijska slowly. "She will see you when the time is right."

I start to realize how hopeless the situation is. My lip wobbles, and a hot tear spills down my cheek.

Mijska spies it before I can brush it away. "There, there, dear," she says, "it's not as bad as you might think."

"Not as bad for me, maybe," I snap. "But what about for Mira? I don't know where she is, or if she's even . . ." I trail off. If she's even alive, I meant to say, but the words are too awful to speak out loud.

Mijska's forehead wrinkles in thought, and at last she says, "Perhaps there's something we can try. Follow me."

We go out of the dining room, down a long corridor, and up a spiral staircase to a door with a brass knob in the shape of a bear's head. I reach for the knob, and Mijska swats my hand away at the same time as the bear snaps its eyes open and bares its teeth. Mijska leans down and whispers something to the bear. It brings its lips back down over its teeth, and Mijska opens the door. I step through warily. It might be a doorknob bear, but its growl was fierce, and its teeth looked sharp.

I step into a large circular room with a high domed roof. From floor to ceiling, the walls are lined with books—old leather books with worn spines and gold-embossed titles. On the shelf nearest me I see *Mediums: From Apple Seeds to Zithers* and *True Tales of the Tsarish Yagas.*

"This is Baba Basha's private library," says Mijska. "It's most irregular for a student to be invited in here. But given your circumstances, I'm making an exception. Now"—she walks to the table in the center of the room—"there might be a way for you to see Mira."

I follow her. "How?" I ask. "What are you going to do?"

"I'm not going to do anything," she says, and she unfurls a piece of paper and lays it across the table.

I step closer, and my pulse quickens. It's not just any piece of paper. It's a *map.*

"I know you're not yet practiced in your medium," says Mijska, "but you can try to find Mira in this map."

My hands are already hovering over the map, but I feel a twinge of uncertainty. "I don't know where to begin," I admit, but even as I say it, I'm reaching out to touch Ptashkagrad.

Right away, I taste gritty, snow-flecked air and hear the loud beating of wings. First, I see snowcapped mountains, but before they come into focus properly, they fall away, and I see flat, frost-bitten plains. The scene changes again. Now I see a city in the distance, and I know it must be Ptashkagrad, but however hard I try, I can't move any closer to it. And then it is gone, and all I can see is a snow-covered forest.

My eyes are watering, and my head is starting to ache. I seem to be lost in the snow, but just as I am about to pull away, the scene shifts once more, and I see her.

She is in a golden cage balanced on a rooftop in Ptashkagrad. Behind her are looming clouds. Before her is an audience of birds; some hang in the sky, and some perch on the roof tiles. She is dancing, but I can see she takes no pleasure in it. Her face is grim, and her cheeks are tearstained. She dances as if her legs are very heavy, dragging her feet along the floor of the cage. But she dances beautifully. I ache looking at her. I have a feeling she has been dancing for a very long time.

I want to see more, but the scene falls away. Next I see an abandoned village, a frozen lake, a windblown tree, the images kaleidoscoping before my eyes one after another. I don't know how to find my way back to Mira.

Mijska gently lifts my hands away from the map. Her touch brings me back into the library. "I saw her," I say, "but only for a moment. I tried to see more, but I couldn't."

"You can't control it yet," says Mijska, "but you'll soon learn."

Not soon enough, I think. Even after just a few days, Mira is terribly changed. She looks gaunt and sad and, worst of all, resigned. Has she given up hope? "I wish I didn't have to learn," I mutter. "I wish I wasn't a yaga at all!"

Mijska raises an eyebrow. I feel myself flush. "I only mean that if I wasn't a yaga, I wouldn't be stuck here. If I was an ordinary girl, I'd be in the Republic of Birds now, or well on my way."

"But you are a yaga," says Mijska. "Simple as that. There's nothing ordinary about you. You may think that is unfortunate, but mark my words, it is not. If you weren't a yaga, you'd have no hope of finding your sister. The Republic is dangerous, Olga. Ptashka III is cruel, and her army is powerful. Without magic, you wouldn't stand a chance."

"So . . . I need magic to rescue Mira?" I say.

Mijska sighs heavily. "You'll need a lot more than that," she says. "But it's a start." She walks toward the door.

"Baba Mijska," I say, and she turns around. "I've seen Mira now, and I don't know how much longer she'll survive like this. I don't have time to spare. What if Baba Basha won't see me until it's too late?"

Mijska smiles. "You needn't worry about Baba Basha," she says. "Her timing is impeccable."

· · ·

The dormitory is a high, narrow room lit by lanterns that cast a thin glow. I see that there are twelve beds, and each one, save for the one closest to the door, is occupied by a sleeping girl. A sleeping yaga.

"There's a basin and jug for washing." Mijska points to them. "This bed is yours," she says, nodding at the empty one. "I'll see you in the morning, Olga, when your lessons will begin in earnest." She creeps through the door and goes to shut it behind her, but then she stops. "We're glad to have you at Bleak Steppe, Olga," she says, "even if you're not glad to be here."

While the sleeping yagas snore gently around me, I scrub myself clean with water from the jug and climb into the gray nightdress I find folded at the end of my bed. It feels so good to be clean, to be lying under a warm blanket. But I can't sleep.

I reach for Varvara's memory bag. Baba Basha may not want to see me yet, but that doesn't stop me from trying to see her. I open the memory bag and dip my fingers into the inky liquid. The dormitory starts to ripple around the edges, and I wander through Varvara's memories: a feast for Tsarina Pyotrovna's birthday; a crowded afternoon in the banya; a hurried carriage ride with the *clip-clop* of horse hooves hard against cobbled streets as the Stone Palace grows smaller and smaller through the carriage window. Sometimes I see Baba Basha, but only ever in the corner of a scene or on her way out the door, and always partially obscured by a rain-speckled mist or haloed with gray storm clouds. Even in Varvara's memories, she is elusive.

Finally, I find my way out of the memories, back into the dormitory and the narrow bed. I suppose I drift off to sleep after that, because the next thing I'm aware of is a hand on my shoulder, shaking me awake.

CHAPTER SEVENTEEN

THE RIVER DEZHDY

O lga?" says a voice in my ear. "Olga Oblomova?"

I open my eyelids a crack. "How does everyone here know my name?" I mumble into my pillow.

"But don't you know me?" says the voice. I rub my eyes and sit up. The voice belongs to a small girl with a crooked mouth and very long, light fingers. I recognize her from the Instructionary Institute.

"It's me—Evgenia Kokoschka," says Evgenia Kokoschka as she sits beside me on the bed and starts lacing her shoes.

"Of course," I say. "You were to be a sextant in the Grand Procession at the Spring Blossom Ball."

"That's right. I was to represent all Tsarina Pyotrovna's great naval advances," she says.

"And then one day, there was a space between Albina and Jelena in the Procession where you were supposed to be. We all noticed. We all guessed what had happened. But no one said anything."

She smiles. "It happened at the Stone Palace, actually, during one of our Spring Blossom rehearsals," she says. "I went down the wrong corridor, opened the wrong door, walked into the wrong room. The door was locked, you see. Locked and bolted. But I just opened it and walked right through. Locks," she says, wiggling her fingers, "are my medium."

"Mine is maps," I say, and I swing my feet onto the floor. "I have to learn quickly. When do our lessons start?"

"Right after breakfast," she says.

Last night, the dining hall was empty and so quiet that Mijska's and my footsteps echoed loudly off the walls. This morning, it is like stepping into a different room entirely. The air is loud with the clatter of plates and the clink of spoons and talking and laughing. The benches are crowded with girls—yagas—eating pancakes, taking turns to plait one another's hair, reading textbooks under the table.

"Are you hungry?" Evgenia asks, and before I can answer, she says, "Doesn't really matter if you are or not. Magic is *famishing*, especially when you're only beginning, like you are." Evgenia tips her head up. "Sausages, please," she says, "and bread and cheese and jam." Rain falls from the domed ceiling and becomes sausages and bread and cheese and jam as it hits the table.

I chew my bread without saying anything, but Evgenia is happy to fill the silence with chatter.

"Maps," says Evgenia while I eat. "That's a good medium. Do you remember Zenia?" She points down the table to a tall, thin girl. "The one who was so frighteningly good at math? Well, that's precisely why she was sent here—her medium is the abacus. And"—she points again—"do you see Katia from the year above us? Well, don't get too close to her in class. Her medium is bees."

At last, she looks at me and says, "You're very quiet, Olga. It all seems strange here at first, but you'll soon get used to it."

I nod. I have no intention of getting used to Bleak Steppe. I think of Mira dancing in her horrible cage. I'm impatient for my lessons to begin.

At last, a bell rings, and all around me girls stand up from their places. Mijska sweeps through the dining hall in a shimmering silver cloak. She looks different—almost stern—as she opens the classroom door.

I step through the door into a vast empty room—or, not quite empty. Along one wall is a glass chest. It looks like one of the specimen cabinets from the Tsarish Museum of Science and Progress, the kind that is usually filled with semiprecious stones or dead beetles pinned to cards and neatly labeled with their Latin names. But this case isn't filled with insect specimens. The girls file up to the chest. I watch as Evgenia takes a padlock off of it. Zenia comes away with an abacus, and Katia with a cloud of bees. By the time I reach the chest, there is only one thing left inside: a neatly furled map. I lift it out.

When I turn away from the chest, most of the other pupils are already at work. Katia is trying to coax her bees into the shape of a pentagram. Zenia holds her unstrung abacus in her lap while the abacus beads float into strange constellations in the air above her. Another girl is muttering grimly at the ink pooled in her cupped hands, though it doesn't seem to be listening to anything she says. It's Polina. I remember her, too.

Mijska moves among the girls, correcting here and encouraging there.

"Polina," she says, "another unlucky day? Never mind, it will come with practice."

She stops and watches Zenia approvingly. "Very nice," she says, "though I believe Orion's Belt is missing a bead."

I find a place clear of bees and ink and unroll my map on the floor. I am ready to begin. I need to find out more about Mira, about how I can find her.

I place my hands over Ptashkagrad and . . . nothing. I wait. All I feel under my palms is paper. I press my fingers so hard into the map that they come away ink-stained, but nothing happens. Nothing, unless you count the faint smell of smoke and—for a moment—the gritty taste of ash at the back of my throat. I am leaning over the map, so close my nose almost touches the seam where the High Stikhlos meet the edge of the Republic, when two pointed silver shoes appear beside the map.

"Now, Olga," comes Mijska's voice from above, "perhaps you are trying too hard."

"My sister is in danger," I mutter.

Mijska gathers her skirts and sits down beside me. "To start with," she says gently, "why don't you begin by focusing on a part of the map that's less . . . fraught. Strong feelings can muddle your magic, especially when you are starting out. Try a more neutral territory." She guides my hands to a blue line that trickles down through the map's eastern part before it meets the Squalid Sea. "The River Dezhdy," she says, "looks like a good place to begin."

I press my index finger to the river about halfway along. First nothing. Then a slimy creep at the back of my throat. I taste something muddy and green and faintly vegetable. I think it's the river. I press my finger down harder, so hard it turns red around the nail and white around the knuckle. Apart from the river slowly rising at the back of my throat, nothing changes.

"I can taste it," I tell Mijska, "but that's all."

"That's something!" she says. "That's your way in!"

"What do you mean, my way in?" I say. I gag on the taste of river and pull my hand away from the map.

She thinks for a moment. "You know, every medium is different, Olga, and every medium must be learned differently. But what's in a map? What makes a map? All the impressions and observations and memories of the person who drew it. This taste—this impression—is what you need to follow."

"Well, how do I do that?" I ask. But Mijska has already walked away. I watch her swish a silvery path through her students, and then I go back to the map. I touch my finger to the river.

Again, the taste of it wells up in my mouth, cold and thick with silt. I want to spit it out, but I stay with it. The taste creeps up into my nose and the smell grows stronger. The smell is harder to pin down than the taste; it dances between a clean, glassy scent and a reek, something foul and brackish. Now and again, I catch the faint tang of engine oil. This must come from the barges that go up and down the river. By the time the Dezhdy meets the Neva in Stolitsa, it's crowded with barges loaded with timber and coal and sacks of grain.

The smell of river water cut through with engine oil reminds me of crossing the Krimsky Bridge on winter afternoons when I wanted to take the short way home from the Instructionary Institute for Girls. The bridge's railing was slick with ice, and the acrid oil scent wrinkled my nose when I leaned over the bridge's railing. I liked to watch the barges, all lit by lanterns in the winter gloom, as they went downstream on their way to the port city of Myrkutsk or out to sea.

I hear the burble of the river and the crack and sway of the rushes on its banks almost at the same time as I feel it: ice-cold water rushing between my fingers and slithery tangles of weeds. The river fills my mouth and my nose and my ears and my hands, and if I can just push a little further—

But as I push, the water slips away from my fingers, and soon I hear its ripples only as faint echoes. My mouth tastes of nothing except saliva. And all I smell is the damp, rainy smell of Bleak Steppe.

The classroom falls back into focus around me. I feel dizzy and disoriented but somehow triumphant. I am starting to feel that magic is something I can make happen. And if I learn to do it well enough, it will bring me closer to Mira.

I go back to the Dezhdy. This time, it all happens quicker. I taste the river, and soon the rest of it falls into place. I stay very still inside the Dezhdy's smell and sound and feel. I notice everything: the soft, clucking sounds of pebbles being tumbled over one another; the croaking of frogs, just like the frogs in the fountains at the Mikhailovsky Garden; the silky feel of the riverbed. And at last I see it, too.

I'm not the only one who sees it.

The other pupils gasp and duck away as the River Dezhdy, fringed with grass and thick with fish and weeds, pours out of the map and into the room.

Soon the whole classroom is filled with silty water, and girls are climbing onto windowsills and clinging to curtains, trying to stay out of its swirling currents. I should stop now. But I have never felt powerful like this before, and I don't want the feeling to end.

A barge laden with logs pours out of the map and hurtles down the river, leaving screaming girls in its wake.

I take my hand from the map. My fingers tremble ever so slightly as the room falls back into place. The other girls stare until Mijska claps and says, "Now, girls, there's no need to stop what you're doing," as if there wasn't an entire river flowing through the classroom not five seconds ago. Slowly, they return to their own mediums. All except for Evgenia Kokoschka. She comes over to me, rattling with keys and locks. Her eyes are shining. "Olga," she says, "you're *really* good!"

I stare at her as her words replay over and over in my ears. I, Olga Oblomova, am really good.

"Olga?" she says. "You're looking at me kind of . . . strangely. Are you feeling well?"

"I'm feeling perfectly well." I smile. "It's just that no one's ever said that to me before."

• • •

At lunch, I sit with Evgenia and Katia and Polina and Zenia. They chatter excitedly, and Polina wiggles her ink-stained fingers to make the others giggle. They seem happy to be here, happy to be yagas. If I had come to Bleak Steppe under different circumstances, I would have been happy here, too. I push the thought away. Soon lunch will be over and lessons will begin again. I will work twice as hard—I won't waste any time.

To my dismay, the next lesson is something called History of Magic. I nudge Evgenia. "Are we really learning *history*?" I whisper.

"Practice in the morning, theory in the afternoon," she whispers back.

I bite back a groan. Theory won't prepare me for the Republic of Birds. Theory won't help me get Mira back.

"Today we are learning about Baba Marisha, the yaga of the Northern Plain," Baba Mijska tells us. "She lived a long, long time ago, when the skies were ablaze with flocks of firebirds . . ."

I look longingly at the glass cabinet where my map is stowed with all the other yagas' mediums. At the blackboard, Baba Mijska drones on and on. I am too busy agonizing over the time I am wasting to pay any attention to her. At last, Mijska's voice breaks into my thoughts.

". . . and took it," she says, "for safekeeping, into the Unmappable Blank. Of course, had they wanted to, the yagas of the Imperial

Coven could have done what neither the tsarina nor the Avian Counsel could manage to do—they could have hatched the firebird's egg. Does anyone know how?"

Mijska's question is met with silence. At last, a girl sitting near the front of the room raises her hand.

"Yes, Nikita?" asks Mijska.

"I . . . I think it's something to do with a feather. If a yaga has a firebird's tail feather, she can use it to hatch the firebird's egg. But it has to be a yaga. A tail feather won't work for just anyone."

"Very good," says Mijska. "And besides that, the story goes that as long as she has the feather in her possession, the firebird will do as she bids. Now, firebird feathers are notoriously . . ."

I sigh and prop my chin on my hands. My gaze drifts back to the map. It's so close and yet so far from my reach.

Later, when night has fallen and all the other yagas are sleeping, I remember that there is another map I can practice on. I creep from my bed, out into the hall, and through Bleak Steppe's labyrinth of corridors, opening every unlocked door and peering through the keyhole of every locked one. I walk through rooms filled with hourglasses and rooms filled with mirrors. I walk down a corridor lined with portraits of yagas. I find a gramophone playing a mazurka behind one door; behind another door is a lake—a real, silt-smelling lake with water weeds at its bottom and whiskered trout swimming in it. I stand in the doorway, gaping, until I realize that the lake is leaking out into the hallway and soaking the carpet.

I close the door and follow a corridor, which soon splits into two corridors. When I take the left-hand one, four more appear. Londonov himself would have trouble mapping Bleak Steppe, I think. But just as I am about to give up and turn back, I see the familiar bear-shaped brass doorknob. I reach for it carefully. The bear's eyes open. It looks at me and snarls.

I pull my hand away. Mijska whispered to the bear before she opened the door, so I lean down close and say, "Please let me in. It's . . . important."

The bear snarls and nips at my thumb. I try again. "I just need to see the map," I say. "If you would only let me in . . ."

My hand is too close. The bear sinks its teeth into the flesh of my palm.

I gasp with the pain, but I try again, and again. I need to get to the map in Baba Basha's library. I just want to use it to see Mira, to make sure she is all right.

My hand is bloody and pocked with tooth marks by the time I trail slowly back to the dormitory.

CHAPTER EIGHTEEN

THE THUNDERSTORM IN THE ROOM OF MIRRORS

At the next morning's lesson, Baba Mijska frowns at my bloodied hand. "Be patient, Olga," she says, "and you'll soon reach your potential. With time, you'll be able to pluck things from the map—walk right through it, even, and find yourself some-where else entirely."

My head spins with possibilities. Of course there's a way out of Bleak Steppe. Of course there's a way to Mira. It's been right in front of me this whole time, and I can't believe I didn't see it.

"I could walk through the map?" I ask Mijska. "And come out somewhere else?"

If I could walk through the map into the Republic, I could pluck Mira out and bring her home.

"Well," says Mijska slowly, "you *might* be able to do that. With a great deal of time and an even greater deal of practice."

Could it really be true that the only thing that stands between Mira and me is a piece of paper?

"Don't try to do too much too soon, Olga," says Mijska. "If you push yourself too far, you'll end up pushing all your magic away. You could lose it altogether."

"I understand," I say. But in my head, I am already in the Republic, already on my way to Mira.

As soon as Mijska's back is turned, I press both palms to the Republic of Birds on the map. I feel paper beneath my hands and the floor beneath the paper, nothing more. But I stay where I am and I wait.

At last, the feeling of paper falls away; I feel air, cold and flecked with snow. I feel myself weightless in the chilly air, and I have to breathe deeply to stop myself from becoming dizzy. I remember Mijska's words yesterday morning: A map is a collection of impressions and memories, and I need to follow them. I stay as calm as I am able and pay attention to the feel of the air on my skin. It is cut through with sharper gusts of wind, and after a while, I feel something fine and misty brushing my face—a cloud. I remember how I passed through clouds with this same feeling of shivering damp as I climbed the ladder to the Center. Sound starts to creep in next: the tearing of wings through the air, squawking and shrieking. I know these sounds. I've heard them over and over again in my head. I've felt them over and over again in the pit of my stomach. These are the sounds the birds made when they came down out of the sky and snatched Mira away.

And with that, the rest of my surroundings fall into place. I smell the clean, antiseptic smell of a winter sky, tangled through with the smell of wood smoke. I taste smoky damp on my tongue. Finally, I see a plain beneath my feet and above me a gray sky crisscrossed with soaring birds. And before me, I see the city of Ptashkagrad and the nests atop its towers and roofs. I know that Mira is atop one of those towers. I start walking.

But moving is difficult. Each step leaves me disoriented, and I have to concentrate twice as hard to stay inside the map. I can't seem to make any progress. I look at Ptashkagrad, and I think hard. Its domes have tiles like the scales of the fish that swim in barrels at the Gribny Street fish markets in central Stolitsa.

The clouds settled on its rooftops look as thick and white as Anastasia's mink.

A sharp pain starts behind my eyes and spreads, ringing through my skull. My fingers are trembling. But I don't let myself lose focus on Ptashkagrad.

The scene around me jolts and stutters and for a moment falls away, and I am suspended in blankness. I blink and concentrate, and I am back in the Republic again. Only this time, Ptashkagrad is closer.

My headache is sharper. I feel weak and strangely empty. But I look to Ptashkagrad again, and I focus on moving forward.

But the tastes and smells and textures of the Republic are harder to recognize and remember. The noises around me grow muffled. Ptashkagrad is closer than ever, but it looks flat, two-dimensional. Like something drawn on paper. I taste nothing. I feel nothing. It's like walking through a void. And then I feel the awful blank emptiness outside of me take hold of my insides, too. It starts to creep through me, winding between my bones, eating away at my thoughts—

Two hands grip my arms tightly. With a jerk, I am pulled out of the map. Slowly, the classroom at Bleak Steppe forms around me again. Mijska is standing over me, frowning. "Do you care to explain yourself, Olga Oblomova?" she says. Her voice is tense. She is doing her best to seem irritated, but underneath it she looks afraid.

"I was . . . in the map," I say. It takes a while for the words to come. I am still feeling dull and blank. "I was trying to move—"

"Well, you were trying too hard," she says. "Don't try to push beyond the limits of what you can do, Olga. Your medium can't be forced. You could lose it. Do you want that to happen?"

Do I want to lose my magic? I am only just beginning to understand it, and already it feels essential. She might as well ask me if I want to lose my limbs. I am trying to find the words to say this, but when I see Mijska's face, I know that she already understands.

"Well, then," she says, and she softens. "Try something a little less strenuous for the rest of the class."

Something less strenuous. I unroll the map and study it carefully. I place my hand over the Unmappable Blank, but predictably, I see nothing. I hear nothing, feel nothing, smell nothing, and taste nothing. I guess my magic only works on mappable territories.

I look at the map some more. Finally, I choose the High Stikhlos. They make a jagged seam along the north part of the map, and I spend the rest of the lesson trying to find my way into their peaks and crags.

At last, I coax a small peak out of the paper, then another and another.

I pull my hand away, and the peaks dissolve. The ground beneath my feet turns flat and steady.

Soon, I have all but lost the emptiness that took hold of me when I tried to move beyond the limits of my magic. But I haven't forgotten Ptashkagrad, and Mira, and that I was almost there.

Around me, the other girls break into chatter and laughter. The lesson must be over.

Evgenia goes past with her heavy lock in her hand. "We're finished, Olga," she says. "You can put your map away."

I stand up and fold the map. "I'll be just a minute," I say.

I hang back as the other girls place their sugar pots and inkwells and birch branches and dolls and bees back in the glass chest.

I hold the map behind me and leave the classroom, keeping my back to the wall. Once I am safely out of sight, I tuck it into my pocket.

For the rest of the day, I can feel the map close to me. I walk slowly so its rustling doesn't give me away. I pretend to smooth out my skirt just so I can check that it is still safely hidden.

That night, I wait until the others are asleep. Then I creep out of the dormitory and down the corridor lined with paintings of yagas. I slip into the room of mirrors. No one will see me or hear me here. I unfold the map, and in the mirrors that line the walls, my reflections unfold their maps, too—hundreds of girls unfolding hundreds of maps.

I'm going to use the map to walk into the Republic of Birds. I'm going to see it and hear it and taste it until it is real and solid. More real and more solid than the cold stone floor I am kneeling on now. I'm going to find my way to Mira. And then—

Well, I don't know what will happen then. But I know I must go to her, and I must go now.

I place my hands on the map, and a crisp wind hits me almost immediately. But I don't find myself in the plains outside Ptashkagrad. I am in a stunted forest that clings to the side of a mountain. At the top of the mountain is a strange building perched on stilts.

My breath catches. It's the Imperial Center for Avian Observation. How did I misjudge the map? My mind fills with memories of the Center: the taste of mushrooms; the cold seeping up from between the floorboards; the warm, sweet smell of porridge.

The map moves around me, and suddenly I am in the Center's entranceway. The kitchen door is ajar. The stove is burning low. Father sits at the table opposite Anastasia. They stare at each other in grim silence. After a long while, there is a noise at the door, and Pritnip steps in. His face is ashy gray, and his eyes have a weary glaze. "I'm sorry, Oblomov," he says, "but it's impossible. Every time we try to push into the Republic, the birds push us back. Do you see?" He wiggles a finger through a hole in his jacket. "My men have been pecked to exhaustion. This rescue mission, it's"—he sits heavily in a chair—"it's folly."

"*Folly!*" blazes Anastasia, staring at Father. "Well, you certainly know a thing or two about that, don't you, Aleksei?" She pushes her chair back and goes to the window. Her fingers turn white where they grip the sill. "It was *folly* to try to find the firebird's egg. And see where that folly led you? You've angered the Republic. And you've—*we've*—paid the price."

Father has sunk his face into his hands. "If I had only known," he says, "I would never have acted so rashly. So stupidly." He is silent for a long while. When he speaks again, his voice is hoarse. "I just want them back. My girls," he mumbles through his fingers. "My girls."

I have never seen Father so sad. It is too much to bear. I pull my hands away from the map and take a deep breath. I know I must try again.

This time, I aim straight for Ptashkagrad. It happens just the way it did in class this morning. I am standing in the icy wasteland outside the city. I can see it glinting in the distance. I will myself to move closer. The map shifts around me, and the city grows closer and closer. But the closer I come to Ptashkagrad, the less I can see. There are blank, empty patches around me. I try to push on, but the longer I stay in the map, the larger they grow.

And then the blankness turns inward, and I feel it creeping through me. I am so close to Ptashkagrad now, but I know I need to stop.

I pull away from the map, breathe deeply, let my thoughts fall back into order. I am about to try again when a rumbling noise shudders the walls of the room and sets the mirrors shivering.

A drop of rain plunks onto the floor. Then another. And another.

I look up.

Just beneath the ceiling, storm clouds have formed. I watch as a storm takes place in miniature in a far corner of the room. Wind rattles the walls, and rain comes down in thick sheets. Lightning forks through the room and the hundreds of reflected rooms, and thunder crashes through the air.

"Come here," says a voice that seems to be made of thunderstorm. I stay where I am in a stupid daze.

"Come. Here," says the voice.

I gather up the map, get to my feet, and edge closer to the storm.

The rain keeps falling, heavier and heavier. I am fixed to the floor. I want to run, but my feet won't budge. I realize the rain has taken the shape of a person. A few seconds more, and the rain stops. A woman stands before me. She is tall and thin with skin the color of frozen water. Her hair is lightning-white, and though the rest of her is very still, her hair crackles with electricity. I have seen her before in Varvara's memories. She is one of the Imperial Coven. Baba Basha. At last!

"Olga Oblomova," says Baba Basha. She swishes her rain-blue skirt and then sits down in a large cloud armchair. "I am Baba Basha, headmistress of Bleak Steppe. I'm pleased to meet you at last. Perhaps you could tell me what, exactly, you are doing."

I look down at the map in my hands and consider making some kind of excuse, but I don't think Baba Basha will easily be convinced by whatever story I might come up with. There is something about her calm expression that makes me feel it is a thin covering for great depths beneath. I can tell that she is not to be trifled with.

"I took the map from class," I say. "I know I shouldn't have. But there's somewhere I need to go—"

She nods. "The Republic of Birds. I am aware that your sister is being held there."

"That's right," I say. "I thought I could use the map to get there."

"You're right, you know," she says. "You *could* use the map to get there. Tell me, were you close just now?"

"I was close!" I say. "But I need to try harder. I need to concentrate more."

"Were you very close?"

"Yes," I say.

"Be honest, now," she says.

I think. I *was* close. But the farther I went into the map, the looser my grip on myself became.

"You're a yaga, Olga," says Basha. "You have abilities you haven't even dreamt of yet. But it would be the work of years to step into a map and come out somewhere else, let alone bring something, or someone, back with you. I believe Mijska has already told you this."

"I know," I say. "But I thought—"

"You thought that if you needed it to happen badly enough, it just might?"

I nod miserably.

Basha's face softens. "If you push yourself too far, overstep the limits of your ability, then you could lose your medium. But you already know that."

I nod.

"And that's why you stopped, isn't it?"

I nod again.

Basha lets out a deep sigh. "I see great potential in you, Olga," she says. "Were you to stay at Bleak Steppe, one day you'd be able to walk through the center of the globe, to spin the world around on its compass points. You'd be able to go through the map into the

Republic of Birds as easily as walking through a door. But there's no time for that."

"No," I say sadly, wishing with all my heart that there was enough time. "There's not."

"And yet," she says, "you've learned where your limits lie. The journey to come will test those limits sorely, Olga. When the time comes, I think you'll know what to do."

I unfold the map and study it. "Where is Bleak Steppe?" I ask, and Basha points with an ice-blue finger. There's so much distance between where I am now and the Republic—and it's dotted with forest, zigzagged by the river, jagged with mountains. How can it be so far away when I was there—or almost there—only minutes ago? I want to cry with the unfairness of it.

But crying won't take me any closer to Mira. I take a deep breath instead. "Baba Mijska says only you can decide when I can leave Bleak Steppe," I say.

She nods.

"So, what can I do to persuade you to let me go now?"

"Sometimes," she says, "all you have to do is ask."

Lightning cracks from the ceiling, and its white flash bounces through the mirrors. For a moment, I can see nothing but light. When my eyes adjust, I see that Basha is holding my coat and hat in one hand and Varvara's memory bag in the other. She gives them to me.

As I am buttoning my coat, I ask, "When all this has finished, can I come back?"

She smiles. "Even if you're not at Bleak Steppe, you'll always belong here."

It's not until she has shut the front door behind me that I realize she didn't answer my question.

CHAPTER NINETEEN

IN THE FOOTSTEPS OF THE GREAT CARTOGRAPHERS

The Bleak Steppe gates swing open, and Basha marks my path through the trees with a bolt of lightning. Gusts of rain-soaked wind speed me on my way and cushion the ground beneath my feet. For the first few hours after I leave, I'm not really walking at all. I'm being carried along in a damp, windy cocoon.

But even when Basha's enchantments fade and my speed slows, I don't lose momentum. I feel, for the first time since I left the Imperial Center for Avian Observation, that I am going in the right direction. But all this forward movement can't stop the small, needling pang of regret I feel. If things were different, I might have stayed at Bleak Steppe; I might have stayed in a place where I felt like I belonged. I might have learned to move through the map with the kind of ease and grace Mira has when she dances.

But I hurry on. There is no place to look but ahead. I go faster. The gentle blur of rain fills my ears, and as my steps become automatic, my thoughts turn to Mira, to her dancing in the cage. Her eyes were harder than I remember them, her lips pinched and troubled, her arms and legs scrawny. The only time I've seen Mira look sad like that was when I snapped at her before the Spring Blossom Ball rehearsal. When I told her to disappear.

I walk through the night, thinking only of Mira.

Dawn breaks, and the sky grows lighter. But the trees become darker and closer together as I go deeper into the forest.

The trees here are scarred, and some are dead and blackened. I am back in the Dead Wood.

I walk until my legs are aching and my eyes are gritty with tiredness. Then I rest, sitting against a mossy stump. The ground is cold and hard, and the moss at my back is damp, but I close my eyes, and in a moment I am asleep.

When I wake, I unpeel myself from the stump, brush away the dirt that has settled on my face, and loosen my collar. Then I take the map from my coat pocket and open it on the forest floor. I know that if I push too hard and too far, I might lose the little magic I have, but my hand hovers over the Republic. If I were a little more skilled, a little more powerful, I could be there right now.

But I'm not.

I turn my hand into a fist and pull it away from the map. I need to find the River Dezhdy in the Dead Wood and follow it upstream into the High Stikhlo Mountains and beyond, to the Republic. I re-lace my boots, tuck the map inside Varvara's memory bag, and pull it tightly shut. I am ready to go northward.

There's only one problem, I realize, looking up through the trees and into the clouded sky. I don't know which way northward is. And I can't navigate by the sun when it's behind a thick bank of clouds. It was all very well for Golovnin to steer his course across the Golden Plain with the rays of the sun, I think, but what did he do when there was no sun to be seen? Did he just sit and wait for it to burst out from behind the clouds again? I lean my head back against the stump and its damp, slimy cushion of moss.

And then I leap up.

Moss! Golovnin navigated by the sun, but when Kovalsky traversed the thick forests of Lodzk, there was hardly any sun to be seen. I plunge my hand inside Varvara's bag and ignore the tug of memories inside—a scrap of music, the smell of strawberries—until

I find *Great Names in Tsarish Cartography*. I flip through the pages until I reach chapter three: "Kovalsky Traverses the Lodzk Valleys."

> *Kovalsky was well versed in the habits of mosses and lichens, and he knew that they tended to grow on the northern sides of rocks and trees. Taking a quick survey of the moss-covered trunks around him, he was soon able to find his way out of the Dread Gorge and rejoin the expedition as it made for its final destination.*

Perfect. I snap the book shut and go from tree to tree, narrating in my head:

> *Taking a quick survey of the moss-covered trunks around her, Olga Oblomova was soon able to determine north and to find her way through the Dead Forest to the River Dezhdy and on to the High Stikhlo Mountains and the Republic beyond . . .*

And, just as if I were a cartographer in *Great Names in Tsarish Cartography*, it works: I follow the moss through the forest until I hear, at a distance, the rushing sound of a river. The Dezhdy. For a while I just stand there, letting the silky swish of the water fill my ears, until another sound intrudes. It is a deep, loud gurgle, and it emanates from the pit of my stomach. I don't need to check the angle of the sun in the sky or the position of the moss on the tree stumps to know that I haven't eaten since last night's dinner.

I reach into the memory bag for the pickled mushrooms I packed. Just looking at them turns my stomach, and I think longingly of Bleak Steppe and its delicious food that rained down from the ceiling. I eat the mushrooms as I walk. If I don't stop to eat pickled mushrooms, perhaps I also won't stop to think about the fact that I'm eating pickled mushrooms. My plan works surprisingly well until my fingers find the jar empty. I check the bag for the silver apple Baba Mijska gave me, but all I find is a handful of silvery dust, and I realize I have nothing else to eat. Kovalsky might have been separated from his expedition, I think bitterly, but he would never have been stupid enough to set out without ample rations. Golovnin, Londonov, Pavlev—none of the Great Cartographers would have set out on a days-long journey with nothing more than a couple of jars of pickled mushrooms. Golovnin took three cases of canned soup with him across the Golden Plains. Pavlev never went anywhere without a month's supply of good rye bread and honey. I stomp my way through the trees to the river, listing in my head all the supplies Karelin took on his journey up the Dezhdy as a kind of punishment for my own failing: a whole crate of pickled herrings and apple preserves and salted beef, which went overboard when the barge collided with an ice floe.

A whole crate of pickled herrings and apple preserves and salted beef that went overboard, leaving him with no more rations! He had to survive for *weeks* on fish from the Dezhdy and forest berries. I fumble for the book and find chapter sixteen: "Journey to the Dezhdy's Source":

Karelin would have starved had he not eaten the cloudberries that grew close to the banks of the Dezhdy and the trout that lived in the river, which he speared with his dagger, a gift from Tsarina Pyotrovna herself.

I weigh my options. I don't have a dagger, much less one gifted to me by a tsarina. I don't even have the arrow Fedor gave me. If only I hadn't broken it against the door of the yaga's hut. Under the frost that coats everything here, there are bright bunches of berries: some orange, some pinkish red. But unlike Karelin, I don't know a cloudberry by sight. I pluck a pinkish-red berry and squash it. Its juice comes out a vivid purple that stains my gloves. I can't risk poisoning myself, even though there are so many other ways I could meet a terrible end before I make it into the Republic:

falling down a mountainside; losing all my limbs to frostbite; get-ting pecked to pieces by birds. I brush the squashed remains of the maybe-cloudberry from my gloves and keep going toward the river. I stop twice along the way: once to pocket a promisingly sharp-looking rock, and once to pick up a long stick.

The river sounds closer.

I see a flash of icy-gray water through the trees.

I will catch a trout for lunch.

I narrate my movements to myself:

Oblomova found it difficult to sharpen the stick, even though she had found a nicely sharp-looking rock for that exact pur-pose. With her gloves on, the rock proved too hard to grip, but with her gloves removed and her hands exposed to the cold, her fingers so quickly lost all feeling that she might as well have been trying to sharpen the stick with a pat of butter. Nevertheless, having sustained only four scrapes to her knuckles and one bloodied thumbnail and having cursed the name of Karelin only seven and a half times, she deemed the point of her stick sufficiently . . . pointy.

Somehow, narrating the story as if it's happening to some-one else makes it seem more like an adventure. I wonder if the cartographers in *Great Names in Tsarish Cartography* thought their glorious adventures were so glorious at the time they were having them or if they only became glorious once they were recorded in a book.

When my stick is sharp enough and the cuts on my hand have stopped bleeding, I pick my way down to the riverbank, lie flat on my belly, and continue the tale of Olga Oblomova.

With great patience, Oblomova lay on the bank of the Dezhdy and searched its waters for a flash of pink trout beneath the gray sludge of the melting ice. She did not have to wait long to see a fish, although after her first efforts to spear it, she concluded that she might have to wait quite a long time before she success- fully captured one. It was not until approximately half an hour and two dozen fish had passed that she speared one through its soft belly—

Wait! *She speared one through its soft belly!*

I scramble upright and hold my stick aloft as the speckled pink fish at its top flops back and forth in the air. I've done it! Just like Karelin!

I turn to the task of building a fire, and this time it's Pavlev to the rescue. Pavlev devotes a long passage in his first chapter to the best method for starting a fire from flint. I always used to skip over Pavlev's chapters, as they are quite boring compared with, say, Londonov's, but now I am very glad of his dull description of how to start a fire, including how to find a flint rock on the forest floor and the exact angle at which the flint rock should be struck. Soon I have a feeble flame. I feed it with twigs until it burns a little steadier, and then I hold the trout over it, turning it this way and that until my arm is aching but the fish skin is bubbling and blackened.

I break the steaming pink flesh apart and shovel it into my mouth. It is spiked with tiny sharp bones, but I think it might be the most delicious thing I have ever eaten. It gives me a warm, full feeling and the strength to follow the river eastward to the mountains.

I set out again, and before long, I start to understand why Pavlev's chapters are so dull. There's a tedium to this sort of journey: moving one foot in front of the other, stopping to spear a trout, stopping again to sleep, then starting all over again.

On the second day, I see a smudge on the horizon that I take to be the High Stikhlos. The smudge grows ever more mountain-range-shaped as I walk toward it, but I'm never quite as close as I think I am. Each morning, I set off convinced that that day will be the day I reach the mountains, and each night I fall asleep, heels bubbling with blisters, telling myself that tomorrow will be the day. By the fourth day, I wonder how Pavlev ever found anything to write about at all.

At the fourth day's end, I collapse on the grass by the Dezhdy's banks. The ground is freezing cold, but I am too tired to care. I find the map in Varvara's memory bag and unroll it. I know I can't travel through it. Even trying is too risky. But I just need to see Mira.

I rest my finger on Ptashkagrad. Almost immediately, I see her golden cage suspended over the rooftops. Birds are clustered thickly around it. There is something sinister in the expectant way they crowd the cage. At last, some of them fly away, and I see Mira. She is dancing, but she looks like a broken puppet. I can't stand to watch anymore. I roll the map.

The next day, the image of Mira keeps me going with my eyes trained on my feet and not on the so-close-yet-still-so-far moun-tains. At the end of the day, I look up. And abruptly, they are there.

Not there in the distance.

Not there on the horizon.

There. Looming right over me, taller and steeper than I could ever have imagined. The High Stikhlos—the only things between me and the Republic.

I lie down in their shadow for the night in a makeshift shelter dug into the side of the riverbank (another of Karelin's ideas), but sleep comes only in fits and starts. I can practically feel the mountains above me.

With the first rays of daylight, I open *Great Names in Tsarish Cartography* to chapter nineteen: "Londonov Summits Mount Zenith."

It's useless.

I can see Mount Zenith, Tsaretsvo's highest peak. It looks like a broken tooth. But chapter nineteen, with its talk of crampons and rappelling, has very little practical use for me. I need to cross the mountain range, not plant a flag on Tsaretsvo's highest peak. But the chapter has a footnote—Londonov took three men with him to the summit, two of whom would return, while the rest of the expedition crossed the Nizkiy Pass into the Northern Plains, where they waited for Londonov to complete his descent from Mount Zenith.

The Nizkiy Pass. You don't read *Great Names in Tsarish Cartography* as many times as I have without learning that a mountain pass is a route through a col: the lowest point between two peaks, the seam where two mountains are stitched together. I am not interested in peaks and heights and summits. I am interested in low, traversable seams. I need to find a path that will take me from one side of the High Stikhlos to the other with a minimum of glory and a minimum of fuss.

I squint up at Mount Zenith, then let my gaze travel down to the place where its rocky shoulder butts against its neighbor's. It is steep. Icy. I can still see more than a hundred ways I might fall from it to a certain death. But I also see that wrinkling through the rock, so narrow it's almost indiscernible, is a path.

I gather my things.

Olga Oblomova set out fearlessly to scale the High Stikhlos' lowest point: the Nizkiy Pass.

I scramble on all fours up the slippery path, wondering how the lowest point of the mountain range could still be so incredibly high. I climb until the sun is full in the sky. Any time I try to straighten up to see ahead, the wind sends me back to clinging to the rocky mountainside.

I climb upward. The slope becomes icier and the wind even more fierce. Twice my feet slide out from under me. Twice I have to claw my numb fingers into the frozen, rocky earth to stop myself from falling. But somehow, I make it to the top. My heart is pounding with terror and with the thrill of having made it.

On the other side of the slope is the Republic of Birds. I crawl forward for my first glimpse of the Republic, and I feel like all the air is suddenly squeezed out of my lungs. I am looking over a sheer drop.

Tears prick my eyes. I've come so far. I'm so close. But from here it's all but impossible to get into the Republic.

Unless—

There's a small crevice in the cliff face. It's narrow and crusted with ice. But—I follow it with my eyes—it goes down to where the rock face smooths out into something a bit less steep.

If I could just swing my foot into the crevice . . .

If I could just inch my way along until I'm in its narrow gap . . .

If I could just reach down to the next foothold . . .

If I could just climb down and plant my foot firmly on the soil of the Republic . . .

It's a lot of *ifs*. I lie there for a while, flat on my belly, considering my plan, and I wonder how this story might be told in *Great Names in Tsarish Cartography*.

Knowing the treacherous cliff face was her only route into the Republic, Olga Oblomova gathered her courage and climbed with calm confidence down the narrow, ice-crusted crevice.

If Olga Oblomova the Great Cartographer can do it, I think, so can I. I stand up and turn around. I grip the rock and lower my body, slower than slow, until it hangs over the precipice. I swing my foot, and I find the thin crevice, and I place my boot in it as firmly as I can. I loosen my grip on the ridge above and slide my hands down to steady myself against the frozen rock face. Then my other foot finds a place on the ice, and I edge along, my face pressed against the rock, fingers cramped and sweating with effort, feet searching carefully for the next foothold. Until my boot connects with a slick of ice and my foot skids out from under me.

I lose my grip, and I swing my foot frantically, but when I bring it down where the rock should be, it plunges into nothing.

And I am plunging into nothing, too.

After the War in the Skies was won, after the feasting and cele-brations and the victory parades through the streets of Stolitsa, Tsarina Pyotrovna's thoughts turned to the firebird's egg once more. She had led her army to a glorious victory, conceding only the barren lands to Tsaretsvo's north to her enemies. The skies above the Tsardom were free of birds; its cities, streets, and for-ests were empty of yagas. And yet, through the deception of her Imperial Coven, the tsarina had lost the firebird's egg. She tried to push all thoughts of the egg from her mind, but as she wrote in a letter to her military advisor, General Stolichnin, "I can't help but feel that the Tsardom would be yet more powerful if it boasted a firebird in its army; our might and strength would be without equal."

She called the greatest cartographers in the land and pro-posed an expedition to retrieve the egg from the Unmappable Blank. But even the boldest and bravest among them could not be persuaded to go. They all remembered what had happened to Londonov, greatest cartographer of his age, when he journeyed into the Blank's icy heart . . .

—Glorious Victory: An Impartial Account of the War in the Skies by I. P. Pavlova, chapter twenty-three: "The Aftermath."

PTASHKA'S BARGAIN

I am falling, splitting the air in two, my skin stretching across my bones and my lips pulling back from my gums. Time stretches out around me. I see the slope falling away beside me and the ground coming up to meet me, and even though I know it is all happening in the space of seconds, I feel like I have been falling for hours.

All I can think about is the head-splitting, bone-cracking *crunch* my body is about to make when it slams into the earth. But as I hurtle toward the ground, I hear a familiar noise. A taut, thrumming sound tearing through the sky.

Birds.

I can't see them. But I can sense them just above me. Hundreds of them.

And then I feel the sharp grasp of claws through my coat as I am lifted up inside a dense, feathered, wing-beating cloud. I am surrounded by birds, and I am—almost—flying.

The ground falls farther and farther away. A startled laugh escapes me. I am surprised at this new weightless, floating sensation. I have never felt so light or so free.

But soon enough, I am hit by the realization that I have been captured. I don't know where the birds are taking me or what they want with me. They fly swiftly and with purpose away from the mountains and into the Republic.

We fly over barren plains, gritty with ice and boulders, until, through the distant haze, the outline of a city appears.

Soon the outline takes form, and I can pick out domes and turrets, buildings, sprawling streets. I have seen this city before through the map. I know that it is Ptashkagrad. I know that one of these turrets holds Mira's cage.

The birds dip down, flying low to the ground, swooping through the streets of the city. They fly like dark, feathered arrows straight into the heart of the city. It must have been grand once. But now the buildings are stained with a century's grime. Their windows are broken. Doors hang ajar. The cobblestones of the wide avenues are choked with weeds.

As fast as we swooped down, we soar up again, so quickly it feels like I have left my stomach behind me.

I am lifted higher and higher, out of the streets and into the clouds.

Up here, the city tells a different story.

Up here, the tiled roofs of the buildings are gleaming. They are dotted with nests woven from twigs and boughs. Some are small, flat, and saucer shaped. Others are tiered like cake stands. Some are the size of small houses. Almost all the nests contain furniture that must once have belonged to the people who lived in the houses below: Persian carpets, tapestries, heavy wooden dressers, and even a pianola.

Up in the mountains, at the Imperial Center for Avian Observation, the sky was wide and—most of the time, at least—empty. Here it is filled with birds. And all around me, I hear birdsong, soft and melodious, swelling rich and warm.

If it weren't for my fears for Mira—and the mysterious swarm of birds that has taken me prisoner—I'd be enchanted by this city in the sky.

I turn my head one way and then the other, searching for a glimpse of Mira, as we head toward a cluster of tall buildings at what seems to be the city's center.

The swarm shoots upward. I see all the rooftops of the city below me. My breath catches as among the turrets and domes I see the glint of a golden cage.

The birds fly lower, heading straight for the cage. My heart stops when I see that it is empty, apart from a thick layer of feathers on the floor. But no—it's not empty after all. I see a girl-sized lump beneath the feathers and a tuft of pale hair.

"Mira!" I cry.

The birds grip me tighter in their claws.

"Mira!"

She bolts upright, and feathers fall around her. She scrambles to the bars of the cage, her hands reaching for me. I reach out to her, but the birds swiftly pull me away, higher and higher into the sky.

Mira is here.

The birds surge forward. Other birds are swooping around us now. There are birds patrolling the skies and sentries on the gutter of every other roof, watching the streets below with their beady eyes.

The largest flock seems to hover over a grand building, tall and white and decorated with rosettes and curlicues. The nest on top of it is woven from shiny, silvery things—combs and brooches and candelabras and snuffboxes—and it is surrounded by guard birds. A bright red banner with a yellow swirl at its center flies over the nest. And smaller banners with the same swirl hang from the roofs all around it.

A voice rings out from inside the nest. It's not overly loud, but it is crisp and commanding.

"Olga Oblomova," it says. "I'm glad you've come."

The birds lower me into the nest, and I land with a tinkle among the silver. Then they lift effortlessly into the sky, leaving me standing between two large black birds.

Before me, a bird perches on a silver throne. She has mottled gray–brown feathers and a sharp yellow beak. She is far smaller than the guard birds but taller than I am. Her eyes are bright, and she has a stern, regal air.

Could she be Ptashka?

I stand with my fists clenched and my lips pressed together, holding my fear tight under my skin.

"Do you see, Grigorski?" the bird who might be Ptashka asks grandly, and the slightly larger and blacker of the large black birds beside me nods its head.

"Do *you* see, Magdanav?" the bird says.

The slightly smaller and less black of the two guard birds nods its head, too.

"*This* is the girl. This is the girl you were to bring me."

Grigorski speaks. "Yes, Your Illustriousness Ptashka."

I suck in my breath. So it *is* Ptashka. I should feel lucky—Ptashka surely has the power to return Mira to me. But I am uneasy, too. What does she want with *me*?

"When we saw the other one dancing," continues the bird Grigorski, "we assumed—"

"The other one looks pretty. And her dancing is amusing to watch, I'll admit. But I asked for the girl with *talent*."

I look around, confused. The girl with talent. Can that be me?

Ptashka's beak curves into something like a smile. "Won't you take a seat, Olga?"

"Umm . . ." I don't know what to say. There is nowhere to sit. But Ptashka waves her wings, and a small flock of birds appears from out of the sky. Their beaks are filled with twigs and stalks of grass. In moments, they have woven a comfortable-looking chair for me.

I sit.

Ptashka's eyes flick over me, taking in my ragged dress, the muddied mink fur at my collar, and the dirt that has settled under my fingernails and in my knuckles. "You've had a long journey," she says. "I expect you'd like some refreshments."

This is not the welcome I expected to receive in the Republic.

"Refreshments?" I say. "Yes, please. That's very kind of you,

Your . . ." How did the black bird called Grigorski address her? "Your Illustriousness."

Ptashka waves a wing, and a gray bird with a long, thin neck glides down from the clouds with a silver platter in its talons, which it sets on the arm of my chair. With one outstretched claw, it proffers the platter. On it are three seed biscuits—more seed than biscuit—and a glass filled with a steaming amber liquid that smells sweet, like honey.

I realize that I haven't thought about what would happen once I arrived here. I thought a lot about the *crossing*: how I could get through the Borderlands, how I would traverse the High Stikhlos. But after that? Did I think I would snatch Mira out from under the pointy beaks of the enemy birds? I certainly never imagined an arm-chair and biscuits.

Ptashka looks at the biscuits and the honey-smelling drink. "I hope this approximates your human food well enough," she says.

"It looks wonderful," I tell her. "Most appetizing." I'm not even lying. Even though it doesn't look quite as delicious as the inexpertly cooked trout I've been eating for the last four days.

"And yet you're not eating," she says.

I have no appetite. I only want to find Mira and take her home.

"Please, Ptashka. You have my sister," I say. "Mira."

Ptashka nods. "And?" she says.

"And I want to take her home," I say, shocked by my own boldness.

Ptashka stretches her wings and puts her face close to mine. "It was you I wanted," she says.

Me? Surely Ptashka is mistaken.

"After all," says Ptashka, "what would the Republic want with a precocious ten-year-old ballerina?"

"But what would the Republic want with an unprecocious nearly thirteen-year-old girl instead?" I reply.

Ptashka looks suddenly crafty. "Ah, but you're not a girl. Not *just* a girl. You're a yaga. We have been watching you."

I remember sitting up in bed in the Imperial Center with *Great Names in Tsarish Cartography* open across my lap. I remember the flutter of wings in the dark outside the window.

"While your family did their best to ignore the signs that you were out of the ordinary, I was paying attention. Where they feared an uncanny kind of otherness, *I* saw potential."

A hot flush of pride rises up from somewhere deep inside me. It warms my blood and colors my cheeks. "Really?" I say, and the word comes out all soft and shy.

"Oh, yes," says Ptashka. "I suspect you have deep, powerful magic inside you; who knows what feats you're capable of? But there's just one feat that I have in mind . . ."

Shadows fall across the nest. I think at first that they are clouds passing overhead. But when I look up, I see that the sky is suddenly thick with birds.

"There's something I want you to do for me, Olga," says Ptashka. "Something I want you to bring me."

She leans even closer to me, angling her sharp beak toward my ear. I sit on my hands to keep from anxiously twisting them together in my lap.

"What is it?" I ask.

"Of course," she continues, "I will reward you. Bring me what I ask, and I'll give you your sister."

A shiver of excitement runs through me. I had hardly dared to hope I would bring Mira back with me, and now it is all but done. I can't think of anything I wouldn't bring Ptashka in exchange for my sister.

"I'll bring it to you, whatever it is," I say. "Just tell me what you want."

Ptashka lazily stretches out her wings, folds them again, and finally says, "I want the firebird's egg."

I gasp. That's impossible. She must know I can't bring her the

firebird's egg. But Ptashka looks me straight in the eye, and I understand that she means precisely what she says.

A sharp wind flaps the flag above her nest, and I see that the yellow flourish has two flame-like wings and a long, straight beak.

A firebird.

Even if I could find the firebird's egg, what would happen if I
brought it to Ptashka? With a firebird on her side, would she start
another war? And then I'm aware of a creeping voice in the back of
my head: With the firebird on *their* side, would my Father and the
tsarina do any different? I shake my head. It doesn't matter either
way. I'll never be able to find the egg.

"I . . . can't bring you the egg," I say. "It's hidden in the Unmappable Blank."

"Ah," says Ptashka, "but I believe you can. It has been reported
to me that you have an ability with maps."

"But there is no map of the Unmappable Blank. And if you've
been watching me," I correct her, "you'll know that my magical ability is quite limited. In fact, if I push myself too far, I might lose my
magical ability altogether."

"And yet you're determined. You will go to the Unmappable
Blank. After all, it's the only way to save your sister."

My shoulders slump. My spine sags. I have never felt so hopeless. What Ptashka is asking is impossible. I can't save Mira.

But even making it as far as Ptashkagrad seemed impossible when I started out. I pull my spine up straight. It seems impossible that I could ever find the firebird's egg in the Unmappable Blank, let alone bring it back to Ptashka. There is no map of the Blank, so there is no way for me to get there, even if I were as powerful a yaga as Baba Basha.

But when I think of Mira, I know it is an impossible thing that I have to do.

"I'll go," I say.

Ptashka flicks her wings again. The birds disperse, all but one. It streaks down through the clouds and lands at the edge of the nest. I have never seen such a beautiful bird; its feathers are bright as jewels, deep blue down streaked with paint-box greens and reds. Its beak is elegant and long, its legs slender. It spreads its wings with a flourish.

"Petrovska will take you to the edge of the Blank," says Ptashka. "If you don't return in two days, I'll assume the Blank has swallowed you up, like the rest of them."

"And what will happen to Mira then?" I ask.

"She will no longer be of any use to me," she says in a chilly tone. "And her dancing will only amuse my army of birds for so long."

Petrovska dips her long neck, and I understand that I am to climb on. I hoist myself onto her back. My hands sink into the waxy softness of her feathers. She tenses her legs, ready to spring into flight, and I turn to Ptashka. "And when I come back with the egg," I say, "you'll give Mira back?"

She looks at me with her small, hard eyes. "When you give me the egg," she says, "that is precisely what I'll do."

Petrovska lifts into the air, and I am carried by her weightless energy. It is nothing like being snatched by a swarm of birds and dragged through the sky. Petrovska flies in a straight, clean line. The wind is fresh on my cheeks, and as we rise higher and higher, the air glitters with crystals of frost. I sink my legs into the warmth of Petrovska's feathers and spread my arms wide, letting the sky fall through my fingers, as we fly toward the Unmappable Blank.

CHAPTER TWENTY-ONE

INTO THE UNMAPPABLE BLANK

Ptashkagrad grows smaller and smaller behind us as we fly over the plains of the Republic. The bare, frozen earth gives way to swaths of feathery frosted grass, then to expanses of deep, crisp, milky-blue snow dotted with fir trees. Petrovska flies on with no sign of tiring, and I am left to my own thoughts. Which are mostly about the egg.

What horrors could be unleashed if I give the egg to Ptashka? I know I'm getting ahead of myself. I don't know where to begin looking for it, and even if I do find it, how will I find my way out of the Blank and back to the Republic? But what if I do find the egg and I do make it back? This is the egg that started the War in the Skies.

Am I going to drop it straight into the hands—well, the claws—of our enemy?

But if I don't, what will happen to Mira? How long can she go on dancing in that cage?

Tears prickle in my eyes. I need to find the egg. I need to try, at least.

We fly on in frozen silence. The ground below grows thicker and thicker with ice and snow. There are no trees, not even small, stunted ones. There is no grass. There is just . . . white nothingness.

But at last, a tree appears in the whiteness. It is so thick with frost and icicles that it looks like one of the chandeliers in the ballroom of the Stone Palace. Petrovska lands on one of its icy boughs, and I climb down from her back and tumble to the ground, sending snow puffing up around me like flour.

Petrovska barely takes a breath before she flies off the branch and away, leaving me alone in the vast white Blank.

I start to walk. With each step, I sink to my knees in snow. I have to drag my numbed feet up out of it one after the other to keep going. The white of the ground is the same as the white of the sky. I look back over my shoulder. I can see Petrovska, speck-like, in the distance. But then snow starts to fall, and she disappears. I huddle deep into my mink-lined collar. It doesn't keep me completely warm, but it does at least stop me from freezing.

I could kiss Anastasia right now—if I ever see her again, I think, I will.

The snow falls harder and harder, coming down in thick curtains. I move forward. Or maybe backward. There are no markers to judge my progress against.

I can feel the cold creeping into my limbs and taking hold of my thoughts. I need to find the egg. But everything in the Blank is the same. The egg could be anywhere.

But Ptashka thinks I can find it. My "ability with maps"—those were her exact words. Perhaps my map holds a clue. I take off my gloves, and with freezing fingers, I open Varvara's bag and take out the map.

I press my hand to the Blank and hope to feel something, anything, but it is just the same as it was in the classroom at Bleak Steppe: nothing. I see nothing, I hear nothing, I taste nothing. How can I? My medium is maps, and the Blank has never been mapped.

I roll the map roughly and stuff it back into the bag. My fingers are numb and clumsy. As I push the map into the memory bag, my fingers brush against something strangely warm. It's the feather Fedor gave me. But it isn't dull and brown anymore. It's a copper color, and even in the icy Blank, it radiates a faint warm glow. It is beautiful, but I don't have time to admire it. I put it back in the bag, and as I pull the drawstring closed, I fumble. Before I can stop them,

Varvara's memories start leaking out, covering the snow with a dark, shimmering liquid, like an oil spill.

As I try to scoop the memories back into the bag, they turn vaporous and rise into the cold air, knitting themselves together, lifting up around me until they form the shape of a palace. It's the Stone Palace—made completely out of Varvara's recollections of it.

Looking at the cold white expanse stretching out around me, I make a quick decision. I walk into the palace. I feel immediately relieved—it is chilly, but the chill is manageable compared to the bone-cracking cold of the Blank outside.

I move through the entrance hall, past shadowy guards, and make for the staircase.

I am heading for the palace's highest turret. Up there, I'll be able to get a better view of the Blank. Maybe I'll see something that will lead me to the egg. But I am soon lost. Sometimes doors open out on to nothing or corridors loop around on themselves, bringing me back to the place I began. The windows look out over the garden in different seasons, depending on the season in which Varvara has remembered each room. A clock reads four o'clock in one room and a quarter to nine in the next. I start to worry about getting lost in the confused corridors of Varvara's memories. I have only two days in the Blank. I can't afford to waste time.

I turn into a shadowy hallway lined with dark oil paintings. I am halfway down it when a door opens and three women step out. I rec-ognize them from another of Varvara's memories: the three yagas of the Imperial Coven. The first is Basha, still ageless yet also somehow younger-looking than she was at Bleak Steppe. The second is the crumbling old yaga with a thin trickle of spiders behind her. The last is the red-haired yaga, Anzhelika.

They walk down the hallway, deep in conversation. And I fol-low them.

"I definitely had it at teatime," says the old yaga.

Anzhelika sighs. "Devora," she says, "if the tsarina finds your nose in her afternoon tea pastries again, she is going to be most displeased."

"Hush." Basha holds up her hand. The other two stop and listen. I listen, too.

". . . if the egg hatches," says a voice.

I stop and turn, but I can't find where the voice is coming from.

"But you know the tsarina wants the firebird for herself," comes another, deeper voice. "She says Golovnin found it on her orders. She believes it is hers."

I look up and see the owners of the voices: two birds, a sleek dark green one and a shaggy porridge-colored one, perched on a gold picture frame.

"But we both know Ptashka sees it differently," says the dark green bird. "We know she'd go to war over it, if it came to that. She's told the Avian Counsel as much."

"Well, as long as the egg stays unhatched, there's not much to worry about," says the porridge-colored bird.

The feathers around the dark green bird's neck ruffle. "It has to hatch someday," it says.

"Beregevoi." The porridge-colored bird has noticed the yagas. "We're not alone."

The birds perch silently for a minute in calculated stillness. Then the dark green bird flies soundlessly away and disappears into the darkness at the end of the hallway. The porridge-colored bird waits a moment before it glides away in the opposite direction.

The yagas lean together in close conversation. I hear only snatches. "Doesn't bode well . . ." mutters Basha. "If they ever found out that we . . ."

"And the egg?" says Anzhelika. My ears prick. "What are we to do about that? If it does come to war, it must be somewhere safe—"

"I have an idea," rasps Devora. The three yagas walk away, whispering together, and I abandon my plan of getting to the palace turret for now. If Devora is about to disclose some information about the egg, I need to hear it. I hurry after them.

Devora opens a door. The other two follow her through it, and Basha closes it behind them. I wait a beat, then follow. This is my chance to learn where the egg is hidden. But Varvara's memories are not exactly logical, and when I go through the door, I step from a hallway at night into a music room bathed in sunlight. I'm in a different season—a different year altogether, for all I know—in a room filled with people.

I search the crowded room for Devora or any of the yagas, but I can't see them. A woman in a pink silk dress plucks a harp. Her delicate music soon swells with a strange, beautiful sound. I look up and see that the rafters are filled with birds, singing with their beaks to the roof. At the end of the song, the people below break into applause. It is wonderful.

I suppose this is what things were like before the War in the Skies, how they might have remained if not for the squabble over the firebird's egg. The harp starts again, and I leave reluctantly—I would like to stay in this sunlit room and listen to this music forever. But I go back to the door and open it, expecting to step back into the hallway. Instead I find a different room. The furniture is crooked. Golden chairs lie on their sides on the wrinkled carpet, and the velvet curtains hang askew. Small knots of people stand talking in tense voices. In the rafters is a small clump of birds, huddled tight. Every now and then, a nervous-looking bird with blue-black feathers looks over its shoulder at the people gathered below.

Loud footsteps break through the chatter, and a bearded man

rushes in waving a piece of paper sealed with crimson wax. "The tsarina has decreed it," he cries, breaking the seal and reading from the paper. "We are at war!"

The birds in the rafters swoop through the room and out the window. People break out of their groups—some stride out of the room, and others rush to the windows. "Look!" cries a woman in a bright blue dress, and she points at something outside. The Cloud Palace has broken away from atop the Stone Palace. A great flock of birds is pulling it away through the sky. Wind tears at its turrets, and small cloudlets break off and drift alone through the sky.

So this is the moment the War in the Skies began.

It feels strange to think that I am witnessing the moment that changed Tsaretsvo forever. Things might have been so very different, if . . . But there's no time for *ifs*. I need to find the yagas. I need to know where they hid the egg. I run from the room, rushing through the palace halls, trying to retrace my steps, but I find myself in the palace gardens instead. It is early morning, I think, judging by the fresh, misty air. When I look up, the Cloud Palace still floats serenely above the Stone Palace. Its turrets are tinged pink by the rising sun.

Behind me, I hear rapid footsteps. Someone is running through the garden, puffing hard. It sounds like she is scared, perhaps trying not to cry.

I turn around and see her appear from a gap in the hedgerow: a small, thin girl wearing a black dress buttoned all the way up to her chin. She has sharp, dark eyes, and unlike everyone else who moves through Varvara's memories, she looks straight at me, as if she knows I am here. Almost as if she has been expecting me.

I have seen those sharp, dark eyes before, though the face they usually peer out from is far older.

"Varvara?" I say.

Before she can answer, she is caught by two guards. They grab her, one at each arm, and drag her back through the hedge. I run after them.

In the distance is another figure, coming closer—a woman in an inky velvet dress. I know her from pictures in history books and images on coins. She is Tsarina Pyotrovna.

The guards drop Varvara at her feet.

"Tell me," spits the tsarina. "Where have they taken it?"

"T-taken what?" stutters Varvara. She gets to her feet. She is trembling.

"I thought you were supposed to know things," says the tsarina. "I thought you were a . . . a . . ."

"A voyant," says Varvara. "And I do know things. I can see things. Only not necessarily when I'm asked to."

"I'm not *asking*," says the tsarina. "I'm *ordering*! Tell me where the Coven has taken the egg. *My* egg!"

Varvara blinks and concentrates. She stays very still. Finally, she says, "I see . . . nothing."

The tsarina slaps her hard across the face.

Varvara reels. She presses her hand to her cheek, which is already bright red.

"Nothing?" shrieks the tsarina. "Do you really mean to tell me you see *nothing*?"

"Yes," says Varvara. "White nothing. Empty nothing. A blankness. The egg is in the Unmappable Blank."

The tsarina goes pale. "No!" she says. "They can't have taken it there!"

"But they have," says Varvara.

"Look again," says Tsarina Pyotrovna. Her eyes are mean and narrow.

Varvara concentrates again. And when she is done, she simply looks at Tsarina Pyotrovna and says, "The egg is in the Blank."

"Take her away," the tsarina tells the guards. "I don't wish to see her again. And the same goes for the yagas." Her voice is rising to a shriek. "The Imperial Coven has already disappeared—see to it that there are no other yagas left in the Tsardom!"

The guards march Varvara out of the garden and through the palace doors.

I follow, but when I go through the door, I enter a small, dark room lit only by a flickering blue fire. Three chairs are pulled close around it, and on them sit the three yagas of the Imperial Coven, deep in conversation.

"Normally," says Basha, "the egg would hatch in its own time. But, as we all know, it can be hatched by a yaga."

"But none of us has a tail feather," croaks Devora. "I lost mine more than five hundred years ago."

"And I never had one to begin with," says Anzhelika with a toss of her flame-red hair.

"Neither did I," says Basha, "but that's beside the point. What do you think will happen if the tsarina finds out that it is within our power to hatch the egg?"

Devora and Anzhelika nod solemnly.

"She won't rest until she has found a tail feather and made one of us hatch it. And if the egg hatches . . ."

"There's certain to be war," says Anzhelika with a grimace.

"There's certain to be war either way, if you ask me," grumbles Devora.

"But if one side has a firebird at its command . . ." says Basha. "I say we hide the egg. Keep it somewhere safe. Lay low for the next century or two."

Devora arches an eyebrow. "As you know," she says, "I have a winter hut in the Blank . . ."

Anzhelika looks at Basha, and Basha looks at Devora. Devora sits very still, but a trail of spiders crawls out from between the folds of her skirt. They creep under the door and disappear. The three yagas say nothing. I watch the fire's blue flames throwing shadows on their faces, waiting hungrily for more. What hut? How can I find it?

The door creaks open. Devora's spiders stream back inside. Only now they are carrying something—something egg-shaped, wrapped in layers of gossamer. Devora scoops it up and hides it in the folds of her dress. She stands up and leaves the room, beckoning the others to follow.

I go, too, but as soon as I step through the door, I find myself on a steeply winding staircase. I've lost the yagas again.

This time, the stairs don't take me away from where I want to go, and the corridors don't fold back on themselves. They take me to the palace's highest turret. I am soon looking out at the Blank. All I see everywhere is white, white, white. White—

And a thin streak of ashy gray.

I lean over the edge of the turret, straining to see what it is.

Smoke. Which means there must be a fire. And where there's a fire, there might be a chimney and a house. Perhaps a hut, I think, rather than a house. A yaga's hut . . .

CHAPTER TWENTY-TWO
THE YAGA'S
HUT IN THE SNOW

I run down the stairs, out through the palace gates, and back into the stinging cold of the Unmappable Blank. But this time I know where I'm going—and I'm determined to get there before the cold turns my brain thick and woolly. The palace ripples, then melts, returning to liquid as I shut the gates behind me. I scoop as many of the memories as I can back into the bag and strike out in the direction of the smoke.

I make out a shape in the distance, nearly as white as the snow and the sky. Nearly as white, but not quite. I double my pace, and soon the shape becomes a small house. As I come closer, I can see its shingled roof, whiskered with icicles, and its crooked chimney.

Just outside the house is a pack of white dogs, snoozing in the snow. Their legs and tails twitch as they dream.

And now I am close enough to see that the house perches on two frost-shiny, cold-pimpled chicken feet.

It's just as I hoped. This is a yaga's hut. And unlike the hut that took me to Bleak Steppe, there's smoke rising from the chimney. This hut has a yaga living in it.

I walk up to the door, but before I can knock, it creaks open, and a ragged voice issues from inside. "Is that a visitor?" it says. "Come all this way to see me?"

It's strange, I think, that the voice sounds so much closer to my ankles than my ears.

I look down. And I scream.

The scream keeps going out into the Blank long after it has left my mouth.

"Come, now," the voice says. "Why don't you come inside?"

I stand there, looking down at the head that sits on the hut's dirty floorboards. It is the head of an old woman, deeply lined and almost completely bald. The head grins up at me with teeth—wooden ones, mostly—set sparsely in gray gums.

"See?" says the head. "Nothing at all to be afraid of. It's only me, old Devora."

Devora. One of the yagas of the Imperial Coven. The one who proposed hiding the egg here in the Unmappable Blank. My heart quickens.

"That's right," Devora coaxes, "just a little closer."

I step over the threshold, careful to avoid kicking her between the eyes as I go.

Devora's grin turns wider. "Ahh, it's lovely to have a visitor—and a young yaga, too. You needn't look so surprised—I have a nose for magic. I can sniff it out. You'll learn to smell it, too, in time."

Inside, the hut is dusty and sheeted with spiderwebs so thick they seem almost solid. The webs are studded with neatly parceled flies but also with other objects—forks and shoelaces and a broken wristwatch—that have been embalmed in their sticky mass.

I feel cobwebs against my face, and I shudder. But even though it is dusty and cobwebby, Devora's hut is warm. A blue fire snaps and hisses in a corner. A bubbling pot hangs from a hook over the flames. It emits a smell that is . . . interesting, if not exactly appetizing.

Devora frowns. "But I'm not really ready for company, am I—not in this state." Her voice lowers to a whisper. A spider crawls out of a crack in the floorboards. Then more tiny, ice-blue spiders crawl out from behind the fireplace, from the kitchen cupboards, from the rumpled sheets of the bed in a corner. They surge toward Devora's head.

Spiders are Devora's medium. I remember that from Varvara's memories. But that doesn't stop my toes from curling as the creatures crawl over my feet and scurry across the floor.

Hundreds of them carry Devora's head over to a scorch-marked armchair by the fire, where Devora's headless body sits, her hands busily darning a sock.

"Won't you come and join me?" calls Devora as the spiders work. "Warm yourself by the fire?"

I take off my coat and edge closer to the fire, watching as the spiders fasten Devora's head to her neck with strands of web. Devora creaks her head this way and that until she is satisfied that it is stuck fast, and the spiders disappear back into the cracks and corners they came from. Her hands keep darning. She hasn't missed a stitch.

"There," she says, "that's much better. Mind you, I won't stay whole for long. When you're as old as I am, you'll start falling apart, too. Now"—she gestures to the armchair beside her—"sit and tell me all the news from beyond the Blank."

I check first that the spiders really are all gone, and then I go to sit in the empty armchair.

Which is not empty at all.

It's occupied by a man covered in a shaggy coat that seems to be made of frost and snow. He is wearing a cracked pair of ice goggles on a frostbitten nose, and his skin is an unnatural blue color.

I stumble back and almost fall into the fire. The hem of my skirt catches alight, and Devora douses me with a cup of cold tea. "What's got into you, child?" she snaps.

"Is that—is that Boris Londonov?" I gasp.

"Ah," she says. "Yes, he does look quite frightful. But you'll get used to him. I'm quite fond of him myself."

I wring my dripping skirt and lean closer to the armchair. It's him. It's really him—Boris Londonov. More frostbitten and icicled than he appeared in his portrait in *Great Names in Tsarish Cartography*, but still—Boris Arkadyov Londonov.

"Mr. Londonov," I say, awestruck. "It's an honor to meet you. I'm a great admirer of your work."

Londonov grunts.

"He's not especially chatty, dear," says Devora kindly.

"But I've so much to ask him," I say. "I can't tell you how incredible it is, stumbling upon him here."

He grunts again, and I lower my voice to a whisper. "The thing is," I say to Devora, "he was supposed to be—I mean, everyone thought . . . when he didn't come back . . . that he was dead!"

"Well." Devora looks sheepish. "Technically, he was. It must be said, my spell work isn't quite as strong as it was in my youth. It's challenge enough keeping my head attached to my spine these days! Let's just say that Londonov *is* alive, but not as alive as he could be."

"What does that mean?" I ask, still trying to understand how Tsaretsvo's greatest cartographer has come to be sitting in an armchair in a yaga's hut in the middle of the Unmappable Blank. "Not as alive as he could be?"

"Put it this way," creaks Devora. "He's not exactly a sparkling conversationalist. But some company's better than none, isn't it, my dear—what did you say your name was?"

"Olga," I say, and I perch gingerly on an ottoman.

"Olga," she says, pleased. "This is Olga," she yells.

Londonov rouses himself. Devora speaks very loudly and very slowly. "LONDONOV. THIS. IS. OLGA. She's a VISITOR."

"Visitor," rasps Londonov. A spider crawls from a corner of his mouth and down inside his collar. "Olga," he says. And then he sinks back into his chair.

I wonder if he's alive enough to tell me what happened in the Unmappable Blank. What happened on his expedition? Did he map any of the Blank? Just imagine if he did—the map of Tsaretsvo would be changed forever! I am leaning forward to begin asking when I become aware that Devora is talking to me.

"I said," she says, "would you like some tea, Olga?"

I nod. Devora reaches for the poker propped against the fire-place, and she prods Londonov quite hard in the stomach.

"Unnnngh." He stirs.

"Tea, Londonov!" says Devora.

Londonov grunts some more.

"TEA!" yells Devora. Londonov hauls himself to his feet and lumbers off to make it. I worry that Devora is going to ask me where I came from and what I'm doing here. I bite my lip and prepare for her questions.

But Devora is simply pleased to have a visitor. She talks about the Stone Palace and the War in the Skies and old friends and old enemies. Her stories wrap around me like the spiderwebs in her hut. She pauses just long enough to let Londonov plonk down three cups of tea and a plate of biscuits before she launches into a long story involving the king of Kyiv and an out-of-tune piano.

As Devora talks, I search the room for any sign of the egg. In Varvara's memory, I saw Devora tuck it, cushioned in spiderwebs, into the folds of her dress. I peer into the heart of each cobweb, into the shadows in every corner. I crane my neck to see if the egg is stashed on a shelf or in a cupboard. But I can't see any sign of it.

I slurp the last of my tea and remove a web-wrapped fly from the plate of biscuits when I think Devora won't notice. I am weighing whether or not to eat a biscuit when Devora says, "And what's yours, Olga, dear?"

"My what?" I ask.

She sighs. "I was just telling you that Anzhelika's medium is mirrors. Basha's is rain. Mine, as you see"—she grins, and a spider crawls out from between her two front teeth—"is spiders. What is yours?"

"Maps," I say. "My medium is maps."

"Maps," comes a hoarse voice from across the room.

Londonov lurches toward me and pulls a piece of paper from inside his jacket. He drops it into my lap. "Maps," he says again. "Here's a map for you."

I unfold the map carefully and study it in amazement. "You did it," I say. "It was supposed to be impossible, but you did it!"

"What's he done?" Devora asks.

"Mapped the Unmappable Blank! Are you sure, quite sure, that I should have this?"

But Londonov has already shambled away. "Maps," he says softly from the corner of the hut where he now stands next to the broom.

"Mapping the Unmappable Blank . . ." muses Devora. "I guess that's what he was doing when I found him all the way out there." She gestures to the white landscape through the window.

I sit up straight. "Were you out in the Blank?" I ask sharply.

Devora's eyes turn misty and faraway. "That's right," she says. "I was wandering much deeper into the Blank for—well, for certain reasons, shall we say. I was charged with hiding something rather important."

"Hiding something?" I say, leaning forward on the ottoman. I think I know what Devora was hiding.

Devora thins her lips. "Oh, yes," she says at last, "it was a very important task. I had to conceal—how should I put this?—an *object*. An object that many people wanted to hatch."

I am careful to keep my voice light—almost bored—when I ask, "Where, exactly, did you find Londonov?" And I push the map toward her.

She presses a blue-tinged fingernail into the center of the map. "There," she says.

"Somewhere around there?" I ask.

"No." She is firm. "There exactly." She points again, then curses under her breath as her finger crumbles away.

There's only one reason I can think of for Devora to have traveled so far into the Unmappable Blank. She must have been hiding the egg when she stumbled across Londonov. There's no better place to start looking than the place on the map that Devora has just pointed to. While she is distracted by the business of reattaching her finger to her hand, I scan the cluttered table, and underneath the plate of biscuits I see a greasy pencil stub. I take it and mark the map with an X and then drop it into my pocket.

Londonov notices, and I see a flicker of understanding light up his eyes.

I trace my finger over the X. As I do, I feel ice-sharp cold. I taste snow. I see white. I pull my finger quickly away.

I look up, and everything is still. Devora has fallen asleep under a mound of blankets and is snoring like the dead. Londonov is back in his armchair, snoring like the dead, too, but technically he is the dead, so I suppose that's how he should snore. Even the spiders are still and silent in the hut's corners.

My finger moves back to the map. I place my whole hand over the X. At once, coldness travels through my palm, up my arm, down my spine—I feel like my blood is on the brink of freezing. Cottony whiteness fills my view. But it's not the blank white I saw the last time I tried to find my way into the Unmappable Blank; I guess that's because the Blank isn't unmapped anymore. This whiteness is bright and real, and I'm standing in it.

I push forward, but each step is a strain. I search my mind for feelings and memories that I can use to anchor myself, but I feel like my brain is leaking, like I'm disappearing.

I pull my hand away from the map. What did Basha say about pushing too hard? I will have to strike out into the Blank for real.

I fold up the map. I pull on my coat and my gloves, and I creep to the door, hardly making a sound, until—

Creak!

I've stepped on the wrong floorboard. With my breath tight in my throat, I scan the hut. Devora is still snoring under her blankets. Londonov is still slumped in the armchair by the fire.

But his eyes have snapped open.

And he is staring straight at me.

CHAPTER TWENTY-THREE

SEARCHING THE BLANK

I look at Londonov.

Londonov looks back, unblinking. He points to the map in my hand, and then he hauls himself out of his armchair and lumbers out the door, out into the snow. I watch through the window, confused, but then he turns and beckons for me to join him. I go outside, and Londonov points up at a star, one that shines bigger and brighter than all the others.

Of course! The North Star. All the cartographers—not just Londonov, but Golovnin and Pavlev and Karelin, too—navigated by it at night. It's very kind of him to show me, but it's not enough; I can't find my way through the Blank with only a star to guide me.

"Thank you," I start, "but—"

He holds a finger to his lips, then takes my hand and presses something into it: something cold and hard and gold.

A compass.

I've never held a compass before, let alone worked one. But I remember chapter eleven of *Great Names in Tsarish Cartography*: "Plozhny's Last Attempt to Traverse the Taiga." It was one of the most boring chapters, because in his letters and journals, Plozhny never wrote about exciting things like getting stuck in quicksand or racing to cross a frozen lake before the ice cracked. But he did write about compasses, and magnetic north, and degrees, and orienting arrows.

I line the compass up so north faces the North Star, then twist the dial so that the orienting arrow and the magnetic arrow line up. Then I turn the map to match. And now I know I must travel south-east to find my way to the X on the map.

I am ready to strike out into the snow when Londonov scuffs through a snowbank, then turns around and jerks his head. He means for me to follow him. He walks to where the white dogs were sleeping against an enormous snowdrift. Now they are awake, yelping and bright-eyed. They run around Londonov and tussle together in sprays of snow.

Meanwhile, Londonov is attacking the snowdrift, kicking it with his big boots and taking wild swipes at it with his arms. The snow falls away in a sheet, and underneath it is a sled.

My breath catches.

A *sled*. It is crusted with ice, but it is a sled all the same.

Londonov brushes the rest of the snow away, and I run my hand carefully over its bow, then up its rails, all the way to the handlebar. "It's yours, isn't it?" I say. "This is the sled you took on your expedition."

He smiles. Then he points at me. "Yours now," he says. He gives a long, low whistle, and the tumbling, tail-wagging tangle of dogs forms into a neat pack of six who obediently allow themselves to be harnessed. Londonov shows me how to jog the reins and how to press on the foot brake to bring the sled to a halt.

I clap my hand to my mouth. "You know," I say, "under any other circumstances, this would be a dream come true. Boris Londonov letting me take his sled out into the Unmappable Blank."

Londonov looks at me, faintly puzzled. But somehow this only makes it easier to keep talking. "Of course, ideally, Mira wouldn't be held hostage in the Republic of Birds," I say. "And you'd be . . . well, slightly more alive than you are now. But alive or not, you're one of my heroes. I've memorized all your letters, all your journals. I've read your account of summitting Mount Zenith so many times I almost feel like I was there with you. And now I'm going to ride through the Blank on a sled—*your* sled."

Londonov gives me a wry, slow smile.

"It's almost like I'm going on a cartographer's expedition myself," I say. "Only I'm not drawing up a map or scaling a mountain. I'm looking"—I lower my voice—"for something that shouldn't be found. But if I find it, I hope you'll understand why I did it—you and Devora."

Londonov points out into the Blank. "Go," he says.

I plant my feet on the footboard. I button my collar tight and clutch the reins in my gloved hands. I turn to Londonov. "Thank you," I say.

"Go," he says again.

I jog the reins, and the frozen ground slides out from under me as the dogs take off through the snow, bounding southeast, farther into the Blank.

I go, and I don't look back—at least, not until the hut is just a blurred, faraway shape. Maybe my eyes trick me, but I think I see another faraway shape beside it, even smaller and more blurred. It looks like Londonov is still out there, watching me as I make my way deeper and deeper into the Blank.

And then it is just me, alone. I feel the wild thrill of speeding through the snow behind a pack of excited dogs. I feel the night rushing by and the snow spraying up on either side of the sled as we cut through the Blank's whiteness.

For a time, the sky is bright with stars. One by one, they start to fade, then disappear. The sky turns hazy gray, then dull pink. I travel on until the sun starts rising, red and small and distant, before me on the horizon.

In the light of day, I see just how white and wide and vast the Blank is—and I sense just how small I am in it. I try to push away the feeling that the Blank is swallowing me up.

I distract myself with practicalities. Without the North Star to guide me, I need to orient myself with Londonov's compass so that I keep heading southeast. I look down at its quavering golden arrow as the sled pelts through the snow.

Londonov's map of the Blank is rough. Its landmarks are few. But after a while, I start to pick them out. A frozen lake. An icy ridge. With each new feature, I can orient myself better, adjust my navigation. As I go, and as my eyes become more used to the whiteness, I pick out things not yet marked on the map. Caves and ice fields. Even mountains and glaciers in the distance.

I stop to let the dogs rest. I stretch. My legs are tight, and my hands are clawed from gripping the sled's handle. I wriggle my fingers until I can move them properly again, and then I find the pencil stub in my pocket.

I mark the lake and the ridge and the caves and the mountains on the map. I'm sure Londonov won't mind. It's only a small patch of the Blank's expanse, but I feel proud to add these details. I try to ignore the spark I feel when my fingers meet the paper, but the excitement charges through my body and energizes me all the same.

With the sun full in the sky, I check the compass once more to make sure that I am going the right way. I should be getting close to the X now.

The problem with an X is that it is easy to draw on a map and much, much harder to locate in reality. My hands are hurting, and my legs are cramped, and I am *cold*—the thin slice of my face that is exposed between my hat and my collar feels like it might fall off.

When I finally get there, the place where my map is marked with an X is nothing but a flat, snow-covered plain. I stare hard at the plain around me, feeling colder and colder. Then I notice a faint warmth coming from the memory bag. It is the feather the smugglers gave me. I take it out of the bag. It has turned from brown to coppery to vivid gold, the color of sunlight. And it is as warm as sunshine, too. I turn the feather from side to side, wondering why it is acting so strangely. But strange or not, it is wonderfully hot. I tuck it into my glove to keep at least one hand warm.

I unharness the dogs, then feed them from the sack of dried meat I find strapped to the sled's cargo bed. Behind the sack I find a half loaf of black bread wrapped in oilcloth. I don't know how old it is and I don't care. I tear off a hunk and chew. One after another, the dogs flop into a panting heap by the sled. I look at them enviously. I want to flop, too. But I remember Londonov's frostbitten nose, and I shudder. The best way to keep warm, I tell myself, is to keep moving. And though this might look like a frozen wasteland, somewhere inside it, under one of its folds of snow, I know the egg is hidden.

I pace the Blank in ever-widening circles, looking for something—some small sign—that will lead me to the egg.

I walk until the sun is low and night is creeping in. I find nothing. And I sink down between the sleeping dogs and into their comforting warmth, pushing my face into their pillowy white fur. And I sob.

It wasn't that I had been sure I would find the egg—but I was, I realize now, *hoping* to find it. There was no hope left anymore. For me or for Mira.

I nestle closer to the largest of the dogs. Night has fallen properly, and the snow is dark and shadowed. I slip into a dreamless sleep.

Long before the sun edges over the horizon, I wake, and I start my search again. I search for hours while the sun climbs over the horizon. My muscles ache, and every part of me except my hand in the glove with the feather is bone-deep cold.

I turn back to the sled. I have now been in the Unmappable Blank for two days. I haven't found the egg. I have failed to rescue Mira.

Slowly, sadly, I harness the dogs, take out the compass, and point the sled back in the direction of Ptashkagrad.

CHAPTER TWENTY-FOUR

THE
FIREBIRD'S EGG

We speed across the snow. The sun is well above the horizon now, and its rays turn the white plains an icy pink. The dogs fall into a pattering rhythm, and I relax the reins. Their panting and grunting and the soft spray of snow are the only sounds out here, and I am left alone with my thoughts.

I set out from the Imperial Center for Avian Observation with no plan at all, just the idea that I would find Mira. I never thought about how I would do it. I just kept going, knowing it was the only thing I could do. Have I been completely foolish? Or perhaps also a little bit brave?

Everything has unraveled, and I am returning to Ptashka empty-handed. I don't know what will happen to Mira. Or what will happen to me.

But if I *had* found the egg, I would be delivering it straight into the hands of Tsaretsvo's enemy—and who knows what harm Ptashka could wreak with a firebird at her side? Surely it's better that it stays hidden. If only Golovnin had just left it where it was in the first place. Stupid cartographers, I think bitterly.

Hours pass before I see Ptashkagrad on the horizon. Soon the sky above me is swirling with birds. I jog the reins, and the dogs go faster, kicking up flurries of snow.

Then, from high overhead, one folds its wings and dives, direct and purposeful, toward me. I tense with fear and grip the reins.

Wings wide and talons outstretched, the bird wrenches me from the sled. Its talons tear at my shoulders, and its wings beat hard as it lifts me into the sky.

The dogs bark and jump up, snatching at the hem of my coat with their teeth and trying to pull me back into the sled. I reach for them, but I'm already too far above them.

As I am dragged higher and higher, I watch them leaping and straining. I shout at them to go back to Devora's hut, but my voice is lost in the icy air.

The cold wind stings my eyes as we speed through the sky toward Ptashkagrad. The bird holds me tight, its talons almost piercing my coat. Its power is terrifying.

Am I being taken back to Ptashka? And if I am, what will happen when she finds I have returned without the egg?

At last, the bird starts to glide. We descend smoothly through clouds and over rooftops, and soon I see Ptashka's nest with its bright flag and firebird banners and its dark guard birds. The birds shuffle aside as we swoop toward the nest.

I see Ptashka herself, and beside her is Mira. My breath catches, my heart skips, and a sob, or perhaps a laugh, rises up from the back of my throat.

She calls out, "Olga!" And her face is a mixture of amazement and calm, as if she knew all along that I would come for her.

But she doesn't know that I have failed.

The bird releases its grip on my shoulders, and I tumble into the nest. I reach for Mira, clumsy and stumbling, but the wing of a guard bird folds out in front of me, pushing me back and blocking Mira from my sight.

"As you can see," says Ptashka, "I've kept my promise. Your sister is here and ready to go home with you. But you'll only get her back if you've kept *your* promise. Have you brought me the egg?"

What can I do? I must admit to Ptashka that I haven't got it. And what will happen after that? I feel certain I will never see Mira again. I try to keep my voice steady.

"Let me see her properly," I say, buying some time.

Ptashka nods, and the guard bird pulls back its wing.

Mira has always been slender, but now she is thin, and she looks weak. And under her eyes are bags as dark and swollen as bruises. Her hair, which used to be dandelion–soft, is like dirty straw. She pulls at the end of her plait with her fingers.

Another nod from Ptashka, and the guard bird's wing spreads like a feathered wall between us. And now my time has run out. *Our* time has run out.

It was for the best, I tell myself, that I didn't find the egg. It was for the best that I am not going to place a powerful weapon in the birds' possession. Maybe not for *my* best, maybe not for *Mira's* best—but for *the* best, whatever that is.

"Well," says Ptashka, her eyes darting from mine to the memory bag, "do you have it?"

I look down at my hands in their snow–streaked, sweat–stained gloves. And I see a bristle of feather peeking out of my left glove. It's not gold anymore. It's the color of molten lava, the color of the center of a candle flame, the color of the brightest coals in the stove in the banya. The color of fire.

And it is giving off sparks!

I look up at the firebird banners around the nest. There are hundreds of them. Hundreds of birds with hundreds of fire-colored tail feathers. And I realize they are the same as the feather the Fedors gave me. The feather they thought was useless is a fire-bird's tail feather.

Ptashka is looking at me, her head tilted to the side, expectant.

Mira twists her plait tighter around her finger.

"Yes," I lie. I feel almost sick with nerves as the word leaves my lips.

Ptashka's eyes glint and flash as she eyes the memory bag.

"Yes," I say again as I pull off my gloves and shove them into my pocket.

A plan is forming in my mind. It's a desperate plan, and I don't know whether I can make it work. But I know I have to try it, even though it might not work, even though it could mean losing my magic. No—there's no point in thinking about it. I have no other choice. I must try.

Ptashka's voice is soft and menacing. "Give me the egg, Olga."

I reach inside the memory bag and take out Londonov's map, and with shaking hands, I unfold it as quickly as I can.

"The egg, Olga," says Ptashka. "Give me the egg." She is staring at the memory bag slung over my arm.

Quickly, before Ptashka realizes I don't have the egg, I spread the map on the floor of the nest, and I plunge my hands—both of them—into the Blank.

At Bleak Steppe, I didn't feel anything when I tried to enter the Unmappable Blank. But then, it wasn't mapped. This time, it's different. This is Londonov's map of the Blank.

As soon as my hands touch it, I feel the gritty bite of icy wind all around me. And a faint, fuzzy noise fills my ears. But I can still hear the flapping of the firebird flags and the impatient rustling of Ptashka's feathers. I concentrate harder, but the cold slows my thoughts. Soon all I can think about is how cold I am and how much I wish I could be back in Devora's warm hut—or, even better, back in my bed at the Imperial Center, piled high with blankets, with Mira snoring beside me and snow falling gently on the roof.

Snow falling gently. That's it! That's the soft, fuzzy sound. It's the sound I heard every night at the Center. The sound we heard every winter in Stolitsa, when the snow fell so thickly that the world was muffled and the city was dusted white. It's the sound I heard when I was making snow angels with Mira while we waited for the sled the day we left Stolitsa for the Imperial Center. I remember the snow angels and the way the snow tasted, clean and cold and spiced with dirt and pine needles, and the same taste fills my mouth now. It creeps up into my nose, and I can smell it, too.

I breathe out a relieved sigh, because I know that I have found my way inside the map.

The nests and flags and turrets of Ptashkagrad have disappeared.

I am in the Unmappable Blank once more. It stretches before me, white and vast. And I know that this is my one last chance to find the firebird's egg.

I scan the vast, featureless whiteness. I feel lost. But I am not lost, because I have Londonov's map. And the whiteness is not quite featureless. At my feet, emerging from the snow, is a tiny frozen thread, so slender I can barely see it. I drop to my knees and scoop the snow away with my ice-cold fingers, and soon I have uncovered a gleaming mound of frozen cobwebs.

I have found the egg!

I tear at the stiff cobwebs until I feel the top of it, smooth and round and cold.

I try to pull it out of the hard-packed snow, but my hands come away filled with nothing.

I try again. And again. Every time it's the same. The egg doesn't move.

Tears are running down my cheeks and turning hard and icy.

How could I have ever thought I would be able to do this? I've hardly begun to learn my magic. And Mijska and Baba Basha told me it would take years of practice before I could use my magic to travel through a map and bring something back. And in any case, I'm not good at things. Not like—and the thought comes bubbling up before I can stop it—not like Mira.

I remember how jealous Mira makes me feel when she dances, how awkward she makes me feel when she dances, how ugly she makes me feel when she dances.

I remember what I said to her just before she was taken. "Just disappear," I said.

I remember how much I meant what I said.

And then I remember how much I love her.

I start to feel stronger.

I take hold of the egg again, and I feel it begin to loosen. But I still can't pull it out.

And then, from the deepest corner of my mind, a new thought rises: I don't need to envy Mira. I'm just as special as she is, just as talented. I can walk through maps. I'm a yaga!

I feel magic coursing through my blood like electricity. I feel bright, brilliant, utterly right. And I know I can do it.

I grip the egg and pull.

It will take all the magic I have, but I know I can do it.

The egg comes free, and I hold it in my hands. I have the fire-bird's egg, cold and heavy between my fingers. And for a moment, I feel the full strength of my magic and my wonderful ability.

And then the white snow and the prickling cold and the sharp, clear taste of the Unmappable Blank fall away. I hang on to the egg as an empty expanse of nothingness spreads out all around me and a creeping emptiness takes hold inside of me, too.

I have done just what Basha said I would. I have pushed my magic to its limit. Have I lost it now? Is it gone? I feel drained and sad and exhausted.

But I have the egg. I clutch it tight in my hands as the emptiness takes over.

Then I blink. Above me is a blue sky, bright with red flags and gleaming nests. I hold the egg to my chest. I can feel it, warm now, somehow alive, and getting warmer. And in my pocket, inside my glove, the feather grows warmer, too.

Mira is staring at me openmouthed. Her gaze travels to the egg. Her face creases with worry. "No," she says softly. "It can't be true."

Ptashka's eyes are shining. Her wings are spread wide, and the shadow she casts is large and dark. She takes off and circles the nest, never taking her eyes off the egg.

Mira tries to break free of the guard birds. "Don't do it, Olga," she cries. But the birds close rank and keep her back.

I hold out the egg.

Ptashka swoops. She snatches the egg in her talons, and then she shoots up into the sky, higher and higher until she is just a tiny speck.

A silence falls over the roofs of Ptashkagrad. I crane my neck, following Ptashka's flight. So does Mira. So do all the guard birds in the nest. So do all the birds in Ptashkagrad. Even the firebird banners have stopped flapping in the wind. They hang quiet and still.

The silence can't last more than a few seconds, but it feels like it stretches on for days.

Ptashka returns, flying low over the rooftops, still clutching the egg. She opens her beak and shrieks, loud and victorious. The sound bounces off the roofs and echoes through the sky. And then, all at once, the other birds take up Ptashka's cry. They launch out of their nests and off the rooftops and spin in wild circles, sending the clouds scattering.

Free of the guard birds, Mira rushes over to me. "Oh, Olga," she whispers. "What have you done?"

"I don't know," I say, trying to keep the tremble from my voice. "But I have something here. Something important."

And I slip my hand into my pocket and into my glove. The feather—the *firebird's* feather—is sizzling hot.

"What is it?" Mira presses. "What are you going to do?"

"I'm not sure," I say as I take the feather from its hiding place. "But I think I can—"

I stop, frozen. A yaga can hatch a firebird's egg with a firebird's tail feather. But am I still a yaga? Or did I stop being a yaga when

I used all my magic? I feel suddenly very small and very powerless under the thick, dark, crowing cloud of birds.

"Olga?" says Mira in a small voice. "Aren't you going to do something?"

"I don't know," I say. "I don't know if I can."

She slips her hand into mine. "You can," she says stoutly. "I'm sure of it."

I'm not sure of it. But Mira's sureness is enough to make me take out the feather.

The feather is glowing white-hot, but it doesn't burn my hand at all. It casts a warm glow over the nest and the city's roofline. It turns the clouds in the sky gold and burnishes the wings of the birds as they swoop and soar. Mira looks at me in awe.

I stand still for a moment, unsure what to do with the feather, exactly, but it is like a compass finding true north. It swivels in my hand, pulling at my fingers, until it points right at Ptashka and the egg in her claws. From the tip of the feather shoots a golden spark, crackling like molten lightning. It finds the egg, and the egg breaks into a shower of ash.

Ptashka stops her triumphant swooping. She hovers, stunned and motionless, in the sky.

Slowly, the ash spreads out into a vast cloud. All the birds fall silent. My breath catches in my throat. This is not how I was expecting the egg to hatch. Something has gone wrong. Where is the burst of glorious flame I was waiting for? I watch as the ash is spread thinner and thinner by the wind. Soon it will be gone.

I turn to Mira and whisper, "I'm sorry."

She starts to answer, but her words are swallowed by a deafening crack. The fine cloud of ash suddenly comes together into a dark, swirling mass. With a loud, wild spark, it ignites with a golden flame that blazes like fireworks in every direction and forms the shape of a huge, fiery bird. The bird stretches its claws, arches its neck, and spreads its golden wings wide.

It flies over the rooftops, unleashing tendrils of flame as it goes. Soon the air is filled with the smell of singed feathers, and the birds in the sky scatter, darting for cover wherever they can find it. They huddle under eaves and gutters. A whole flock takes shelter behind the broken clockface of an abandoned clock tower.

But Ptashka tears after the firebird as it soars above the domes of Ptashkagrad. With each beat of its wings, ashes and flame fall from the sky. The clouds are alight, streaked with orange and gold. The city's yellow-and-crimson flags and banners flap brightly in the firebird's wake.

It is glorious to watch. I am elated. But when I turn to Mira, she is white with fear.

"Oh, Olga," she says, "what have you done?"

"I've hatched the firebird," I say triumphantly. "I am a yaga, and I have hatched the firebird."

"Hatched?" she whispers. "Unleashed, more like. What's going to happen now?"

What *is* going to happen now?

The feather glows in my hand.

"What happens now?" I repeat Mira's question to her. "What happens now is that I'm going to use this feather . . ."

Mira looks up at me expectantly. The fear on her face is gone, replaced with a look of confidence. *I* don't know what I'm going to do, but she trusts me.

I start again. "I'm going to use this feather to . . . to . . ." I don't know how I'm going to do it, but I'm going to tame the firebird.

The feather is alight in my hand, sparking and sizzling. I brandish it toward the sky and hope for the best. It makes a pretty trail of sparks as I wave it, but nothing more.

If only the feather were a map, I think desperately, then I would know what to do. I would wrap my hand tight around it and think of the Imperial Center, right down to the smallest details: the way the ice blooms on the windows on freezing mornings; the way the kitchen smells like mushroom soup; the way Father paces the observation deck; the way Anastasia's diamonds and pearls jangle when she walks. And then, patiently, I would ask the firebird to take me there.

Mira grabs at my elbow, jolting me out of my thoughts. "Look!" she breathes.

The firebird makes a wide circle in the sky and flies toward us, exploding the air with flames. It lands in the middle of Ptashka's nest and looks at me with one golden eye. And I know it has understood what I want from it.

It dips its neck down low, and I leap onto its back. I turn to call Mira, but she is cowering at the edge of the nest.

"Mira," I say. From the corner of my eye, I see Ptashka, a dark, distant shape coming toward us. "Come *on*, Mira!" I shout.

But Mira shakes her head. The firebird is huge, bigger than a house, and it glows molten red. And even though it has let me onto its back, there is nothing tame or gentle about it. It is a wild creature, the wildest I have ever seen.

Given the choice, I wouldn't ride a firebird, either. But Ptashka is much closer now. We don't have a choice.

"Come with me, Mira," I call. "You'll be safe. It doesn't burn."

It's true. Sitting astride the firebird feels the same as holding its tail feather—there is a glow of white heat all around, but the feathers don't burn me.

Mira just keeps shaking her head. Her eyes are glossy with tears.

Ptashka is close now—I can hear her shrieks of rage.

I hold out my hand to Mira. She finally reaches out to me as Ptashka lands on the nest's edge. I grab her arm as the firebird launches into the air, and I haul her up behind me.

Riding the firebird is like riding a streak of quicksilver, a meteorite burning through the atmosphere. Mira clings tightly to me while the sky blurs around us and the ground recedes to nothing below.

Ptashka chases us, flying faster than I ever thought possible. She darts and dives as she tries to catch one of the firebird's feathers in her beak.

The firebird lets out a low, angry shriek, then turns its head back. From deep in its throat, I hear the same flinty, rumbling noise that Masha made in the banya, and I know what's coming next.

"Get down," I hiss to Mira as the firebird unleashes a tongue of flame at Ptashka from her beak.

Ptashka, scorched, retreats with a bloodcurdling screech, and we fly farther and farther into the sky, leaving her smaller and smaller behind us. Soon it's like she was never there at all.

The firebird settles into a steady rhythm, flying with deep, powerful beats of its wings. Behind us burns a trail of golden flame and glowing cinders.

Soon the Republic of Birds is far away. The High Stikhlos and the Borderlands unfurl below us like a patchwork blanket. Mira's arms are tight around my waist. I can feel her leaning into the space between my shoulder blades. I have never been so happy.

Afternoon stretches into evening, and the sky mellows.

I turn to Mira. "We must keep all of this to ourselves," I say.

"But, Olga," she says, "I want to tell everyone what you did. You were heroic."

I feel myself flush.

"You saved me. You found the firebird's egg in the Unmappable Blank," she says. "And you kept it from Ptashka's clutches."

"But you can't tell anyone, Mira," I say. "You mustn't. And you mustn't tell anyone what I did with the map, either."

"It was magic, wasn't it?" she says, and I nod yes.

"Olga," she says, "it was *wonderful*."

"Well," I say, "it's done now. I won't be able to do that, or anything like it, ever again."

Mira wraps her arms around me even tighter. "It was still *wonderful*," she says in a muffled voice, and I fill with pride.

She's right. It was wonderful.

We fly on, leaving a streak of fire across the sky.

"But where are we now, Olga?" Mira asks. "How will we find our way to the Center?"

I reach to my waist and take her hand tight in my own. With my other hand, I take Londonov's map from my pocket. I'm sad when my fingers touch it and there's no spark, no shiver of cold, no sharp taste of pine. Nothing.

But in my other hand, I feel Mira's curled fingers and her warm palm.

"Don't worry," I tell her. "I know the way."

CHAPTER TWENTY-FIVE

MIRA DANCES AGAIN

We soar over the Between and the Borderlands. I lean in close to the firebird, urging it toward the Center. I hardly need the map. I have it all inside my head. Soon the forest beneath us gives way to shale slopes. At last, the Imperial Center for Avian Observation appears through swirling clouds. I sink into the softness and warmth of the firebird's flame feathers. "Enough, now," I say. "Let us down. We're here."

The firebird circles the Center and lands in a clearing behind the banya. I'm worried that its bright streak through the sky has been seen—I shudder to imagine what Father might plan if he thought he could command the firebird. But no one comes to the windows at the Imperial Center, and no curtain twitches at the Beneficent Home, either. A muffled crashing sound comes from the banya—probably just coals popping in the stove.

I sink my hands into the firebird's sparkling flame feathers and marvel once more at their softness and gentle warmth. "Thank you," I say.

Mira flings her arms around the firebird's neck. "Thank you," she says over and over, her voice muffled by feathers. "Thank you, thank you, thank you."

The firebird launches up and flies away—away from us, away from the Republic, and toward the deserted plains of the Infinite Steppe. It seems the firebird knows which way home is, too.

I clutch the glowing tail feather tight in my hand as the firebird's bright trail of crackling flame disappears into the distance and the cinders and smoke it leaves behind scatter on the wind. Then, with trembling legs, Mira and I climb the ladder up to the Center.

We walk into the parlor. Everything is quiet and still.

Anastasia is standing with her back to us, tending the fire. She turns when she hears us come in. At first, she does nothing, says nothing. She stands perfectly still, as if she is in a dream and the slightest movement will jolt her out of it. She looks tired. Her face is thin and worn, and her cheeks are blotchy, like she has been crying. I suppose we must look different, too. I know my hair is matted with dirt and my face is grimy and my clothes are stained and torn and singed. And Mira is thin and exhausted.

And then Anastasia breaks out sobbing. "Aleksei! Aleksei! They're here!" she calls, and she falls into a half swoon while at the same time scooping us both into the tightest embrace I have ever felt.

Suddenly, the Center is bustling with activity. Anastasia weeps even more than she did at the end of *The Weeping Woman at the Window*. Father keeps finding excuses to reach out and touch me. I think he is checking to make sure that it's really me, that I'm really here. At some point, the ladies of the Beneficent Home arrive, and they ply us with samovar after samovar of sweet tea and more mushroom soup than I ever wish to see again.

After a while, the attention is suffocating, and I am glad to creep off by myself to the banya, where Masha greets me with a hug.

"I worried so," she sniffles. "I barely slept while you girls were gone. I don't think anyone did. But I never lost faith." She wipes her eyes with her ragged skirt. "I always knew you'd come home." She steps back and wrinkles her brow. "But what a *state* you're in!" she gasps, and immediately fills a bucket with water. "It'll take two stoves of water to get you clean," she says happily.

As Masha sloshes water and snaps kindling, I tuck the firebird's tail feather into the memory bag. It is still glowing, and I hope Masha hasn't noticed it. I peel off my clothes, and for the first time since I left the Center, I let myself take stock of every scratch, every scrape, every bruise, every ache. My journey is written all over my body.

Masha ladles water over the stove, and a cloud of steam arises, warm and pine-scented. The knots in my muscles start to unravel. The tension eases in my joints. Masha brings a dish of soapy water, and while I scrub myself, she works through the tangles in my hair.

It takes so long to get me clean that the fire in the stove burns low. With a throat-clearing noise, Masha bends over it and belches out a neat cloud of flame. Then she turns to me and, through a cloud of ash, says, "I suppose you're not so much impressed by that any-more." Her eyes twinkle. "Once you've ridden a firebird, my own modest fire-breathing must seem quite tame."

I stiffen. We were seen after all. "Masha," I warn, "you can't tell anyone. If Father found out, or Pritnip—"

"I won't tell anyone," she says, and then she shrugs. "Besides, who'd believe me if I did?"

She spills another dish of warm, soapy water over my shoulders. "But I have to tell you, Olga: That golden bird lighting up the sky, and you astride it, your face aglow—you were *glorious*." She takes my hand in hers and starts working at the dirt embedded under my fin-gernails with a scrubbing brush. "I always knew you were . . . that way," she says.

"A yaga, you mean?" I ask.

She nods. "I only have a pinch of magic myself," she says, "but I have enough to recognize it when I see it in someone else."

I look down. "But I lost my magic, Masha. I'm not a yaga anymore. I'm back to being the way I was before. Ordinary Olga."

Masha clicks her tongue. "Not a yaga? And I suppose if I lost the ability to do this"—she clicks her fingers, and a spray of glistening soap bubbles appears in the air—"then I'd just stop being a bannikha!"

"Well . . . wouldn't you?" I ask.

She looks crafty. "Tell me this, then," she says. "Did that firebird just appear out of nowhere?"

"No," I say. "It hatched. Out of an egg."

"And who hatched it?" she asks.

"Well . . . I did."

"And do you suppose anyone but a yaga could have hatched that egg?"

"No," I say.

"And do you suppose anyone but a yaga could have hopped up onto the firebird's back and ridden it home?"

"Well . . . probably not." I feel the start of a smile at the corners of my mouth.

"You're a yaga, Olga," she says. "A yaga is simply what you are. You might have lost your ability with maps, but magic will always be a part of who you are. Now, put out your foot, Olga dear—I've just seen the state of your toenails. Anyone would think you'd walked into the Republic barefoot!"

Later that afternoon, I sit with Father and Pritnip on the observation deck, and I tell them the story of my journey into the Republic from beginning to end. Well, I leave out some parts. Like the bit where I was carried by a yaga's hut to the Bleak Steppe Finishing School for Girls of Unusual Ability, and the bit where I learned magic. And the part where I ventured into the Unmappable Blank to search for the firebird's egg. I certainly don't tell them about *finding* the firebird's egg, hatching it, or riding the firebird out of the Republic.

So it might be more accurate to say that I sit with Father and Pritnip on the observation deck and tell them a few carefully chosen anecdotes extracted from my journey.

Nevertheless, they are pleased with my account, and Father writes it all down in an intelligence briefing and sends it to Tsarina Yekaterina at the Stone Palace. And Tsarina Yekaterina is pleased, too. So pleased that, later that evening, Father receives a telegram:

TSARINA YEKATERINA CHARGES ME TO CONGRATULATE YOU

ON FIRST-RATE INTELLIGENCE STOP OBLOMOV YOU HAVE

EXCEEDED EXPECTATIONS AS CHIEF AVIAN INTELLIGENCE
OFFICER STOP IN REWARD HER IMPERIAL HIGHNESS WISHES
TO REINSTATE YOU AS CHIEF ARCHITECT OF SKY METRO STOP
A MILITARY ESCORT WILL ACCOMPANY YOU BACK TO STO-
LITSA AT YOUR EARLIEST CONVENIENCE STOP RESPECTFULLY
YOURS IMPERIAL UNDERSECRETARY IVAN DEMENTIEVSKY

Father reads it to us at the dinner table. Anastasia makes him
repeat it three times.

When he finishes, she weeps into her soup, and through her
hiccups and tears, she says, "At last! At last, we're going home!" She
is so happy that I almost feel happy, too.

And now the day is here. We're finally leaving the Imperial Center
for Avian Observation and going home. Though Stolitsa doesn't
feel like home to me. But if Stolitsa isn't home, where is? The Center, where there's nothing to eat except mushrooms? Bleak Steppe,
where yagas learn to use their magical abilities? I think for a while
of what I could have learned if I *had* stayed there, but then I push
the thought away. I used my magic to save Mira—what better use for
magic could there be?

There is a knock at the door, and I feel a tugging pain in my chest.
Is the escort here already?

Anastasia rushes to answer the knocking. She has hovered by the window all day with a smile dancing on her lips. She can't wait to leave.

She manages to keep the smile on her face when the door opens to Glafira, Luda, and Varvara instead of the soldiers she was hoping for.

"We've come to say goodbye," says Glafira.

"And to wish you a pleasant journey," adds Luda.

"Oh, the journey will be pleasant enough," says Varvara, "except for a two-hour delay at Strezhevoy and an inexplicably bad odor in the train carriage."

"Oh, dear," says Anastasia. "I do hope there's some way to avoid the bad odor."

"There isn't," says Varvara firmly. "In fact—"

Anastasia quickly interjects. "Would you care for tea?" she says.

Soon the ladies are seated and supplied with tea.

"We'll certainly miss you," says Luda. She looks at Mira and me. "You've only just gotten back, and now you're leaving again."

"It's a miracle you got back at all," says Glafira darkly. "We thought for certain you were lost."

"It wasn't a miracle," says Mira. "It was Olga."

I look down into my teacup so no one sees me blush.

"Oh, Olga," sighs Luda. "It seems impossible. Pritnip and his soldiers tried and tried to bring Mira back—and you succeeded where they failed! I can't think how you did it."

"I can," says Varvara with a satisfied smile.

Thankfully, no one seems to hear her.

Then Glafira, fiddling with the handle of her teacup, shyly begins to ask, "We did wonder . . ."

"Yes?" asks Anastasia.

"We did wonder . . ." Glafira begins again.

"If perhaps," continues Luda, "Mira wouldn't mind—it's just that we'll miss her dancing so, and—"

Here Luda stops, because Mira is already on her feet and clearing a space in the middle of the room.

And then she dances. She waves her arms this way and that, head swaying like a flower on a stalk, and she leaps into the air and hangs there so long it's more like she's floating. She flies like she's a bird.

Luda and Glafira and Anastasia all *ooh* and *aah*. I find myself gritting my teeth, trying to keep the familiar acid of envy from rising up in my throat. But how can I be envious of Mira now? How can I resent her after everything I did to save her?

"Oh," says Varvara, "the two are quite compatible."

I place my tea on the table and turn to her. "What do you mean?" I ask.

She waves a hand airily. "Love. Envy. One doesn't magically cancel out the other, you know."

"And envying someone doesn't mean you don't love them," I say dully. "I suppose you're right."

"Well, of course I'm right," she says. "I'm not in the habit of being wrong. And I expect you're feeling especially envious right now, Olga."

I make my voice low. "It's just that for so long, I thought Mira was the only special one, the only talented one. And then I finally found something I was good at—*great* at. But now it's gone." I fiddle with the hem of my skirt. "I don't know if I'm still a—"

"Yes, yes," she says impatiently. Then she whispers, "Of course you're still a yaga, just as Masha told you. Besides, there's more than one kind of magic. And there's no need to tell me you don't know if you want to go back to Stolitsa because you don't feel you fit in there now. Be honest, Olga—did you fit there to begin with?"

I shake my head.

"You're a yaga," she says again, "and that will never change. So if you feel you don't fit somewhere"—she takes my wrist—"change it until it fits you."

There is a flurry of noise and activity under the window. Mira stops mid-arabesque. Anastasia rushes to the door. "They're here!" she calls. "Aleksei, they're here at last!"

Varvara still holds my wrist. "You don't need to fit Stolitsa," she says urgently. "Stolitsa needs to fit you."

I thank Varvara and ease my wrist out of her grip. I am putting my arm into the sleeve of my coat when I realize I still have her memory bag. "Varvara," I say, and I hand it over. "Thank you—it was very helpful. More helpful than you imagined."

"It was exactly as helpful as I knew it would be, thank you, Olga," she says, and she takes the bag. She opens it and inspects its contents. "Here," she says, checking to make sure no one is watching before she gives me the firebird's tail feather. It has dulled now to the same ordinary brown it was when I first saw it at the feather smugglers' camp, but I'm sure I can still see a faint glow around its edges.

"Keep it," says Varvara. "You never know when it might be useful."

I slip the feather into my pocket. Anastasia and Father are already at the bottom of the ladder, and Mira is climbing down, too. I turn to leave, when Varvara cries, "Wait! These too, Olga. These are yours." She takes Londonov's map and compass out of the memory bag.

I unfold the map and turn it over in my hands. It *is* Londonov's map, but it has my marks and notes and changes on it, too. I put it in my pocket with the compass and the feather.

"I'm sure you'll know what to do with them," Varvara says as I start down the ladder.

EPILOGUE

HOME

Since our return to Stolitsa six days ago, Father has been busy redrafting plans for the Sky Metro. He is in Tsarina Yekaterina's favor once more, and this time we all hope he will stay there. Mira has been just as busy rehearsing for her role in Diazhilov's new ballet. Anastasia keeps herself occupied, too, mostly with running her fingers over her mahogany tables and her mother-of-pearl combs and her porcelain salt shakers as if she is trying to convince herself that they are real—that she is really, truly back in Stolitsa.

Today I am sitting in the Floating Birch Forest Tea Room, high above Stolitsa's rooftops. The walls of the tea room are lined with mirrors that reflect the steaming samovars and the white-jacketed waiters steering cake trolleys between tables. Each mirror's reflection is thrown back by the mirror opposite, so the steam and trolleys and tables stretch out to infinity, and the Floating Birch Forest Tea Room seems to contain the whole world. Though the world I know now is far bigger and wilder and stranger than anything the Floating Birch Forest Tea Room could hold.

Across the table from me, snapping her fingers for service, sits Anastasia. Once she has secured the attention of a waiter, she turns back to me.

Her lips are twitching. She can't contain the smile that breaks over her face. "Oh, it's too wonderful, Olga!" She reaches across the table in a jangle of bracelets and clutches my hand. "I've spoken this very morning with Boris Lavrov," she goes on, "and Studio Kino-Otleechno has decided to make a movie. Of us!"

"What do you mean?" I say, reaching for another cake. "Of us?"

"Is that your third cake, Olga? We haven't been here more than ten minutes!"

I blow on my tea and ignore her comment about the cake.

"It's a most cinematic story, you must agree," she continues. "It begins with exile, with Stolitsa's most graceful Spring Blossom being ripped away from the city and sent, along with her family— handsome father, charming younger sister, elegant, admired, beautiful stepmother—"

"Modest stepmother," I mutter into my cup.

"—into exile in the Borderlands! Though they'll use a studio set for the Borderlands, of course. Disaster strikes when the younger sister is kidnapped by birds, and—well, then the story will follow your adventure. Boris Lavrov says Studio Kino-Otleechno is convinced it will be a smash hit! And why not? It's got everything!"

I smile to myself—neither Anastasia nor Studio Kino-Otleechno knows the half of it.

"Of course," Anastasia continues, "it could have ended later, when your father was officially pardoned, or when we returned to Stolitsa, or when Mira made her debut performance in Diazhilov's new ballet."

"What are they planning to call this movie?"

"Well"—she smiles—"the working title is *Travels in the Land of the Birds: The Tale of a True Heroine.*"

"A true heroine?" I ask. "Is that referring to—"

"To you, Olga! You're the heroine, of course! Though, technically, it refers to me."

"I don't understand."

"Well"—she plucks at a strand of pearls around her neck and looks down at them, smiling—"Lavrov says that with the right lighting and makeup, I can pass for a much younger woman, and . . . he's offered *me* the part of Olga. I'm to play you! In my long-awaited comeback to Tsaretsvo's silver screen! Isn't that exciting? What do you think?"

Anastasia is just as exasperating now as she was before we were exiled, before I went into the Republic of Birds—but when I think of how I used to resent her, I feel ashamed. I remember how she cut up her snow-white mink so I could stay warm on my journey.

Now she is studying my face carefully, almost anxiously, waiting for my reaction.

"I think that's wonderful," I say warmly.

"It is wonderful, isn't it?" she says. "And it's wonderful that Aleksei is head architect at the Sky Metro again—two weeks, he says, and they'll be ready to open. And it's wonderful that Mira is rehearsing for her first part with Diazhilov's ballet company. And you, Olga," she says brightly, "you're just . . . just wonderful, too."

Anastasia can't think of anything particularly special about me, but I don't mind. I know what I'm capable of doing—and I know just what I'm going to do next, too.

After our tea and cakes, we ride back through the streets of Stolitsa. I watch the buildings through the window of our taxi. As we pass the Imperial Society for Cartography, I press my hand against the window, as if I could touch it through the glass. Before we left Stolitsa for the Imperial Center for Avian Observation, I could never have imagined walking through those gates. But since then, I've done all kinds of things beyond what I could imagine. And tomorrow, I'm going to walk right through those gates and knock on the door.

• • •

Later, in my bedroom, I take Londonov's map out from under my pillow and press my hand to it. I feel—nothing. Just paper, dull and flat. I'll never feel a map come to life beneath my hands again, never travel through a map to a distant place.

But I'm still a yaga. And though my magic might take a more ordinary form now, I'm sure it's still there.

I take out the second paper that is folded under my pillow and spread it open across the bed. It is a good map, and it is just about finished. It shows part of the outline of the Unmappable Blank with the landmarks Londonov plotted and the features I found, too. It charts, for the first time, the Between, the place between the Borderlands of the Tsardom and the Republic. It shows Ptashkagrad and the surrounding plains, the High Stikhlos, the Low Stikhlos, the Infinite Steppe, and the winding River Dezhdy. There is a neat border around its edge and a compass rose in the corner. All that is missing is a title.

I lean over the paper, and across the top I write: *Map of a Journey into the Republic of Birds.*

There. I hold it up. Still, I'm not quite satisfied. I bend down to write three more words in the map's bottom corner:

Olga Oblomova, cartographer.

ACKNOWLEDGMENTS

Thank you to everyone at Text, with special thanks to Jane Pearson, whose wise and inspired edits were my map through this book. Thank you to everyone at Abrams, especially Erica Finkel, for seeing the potential in Olga's story. And, for their brilliant cover design and illustration, thank you Marcie Lawrence and Karl James Mountford.

Thank you to Catherine Drayton and Claire Friedman at Inkwell for their invaluable guidance.

Thank you to the School of Communication and the Arts at the University of Queensland, especially Dr. Kim Wilkins and Dr. Natalie Collie.

Thank you to my writerly friends in Berlin: Jane, Sharon, Som-Mai, Anna, Sarah, Dunja, Jan, Tihana, Erin, and Lesley.

Thank you, Miller family, for reading and/or encouraging this story, and to Charlotte for her maps.

This book was written over many years and in many different parts of the world, but one person was with me through all of it—thank you, Tim.